"What did you do?" she asked. The whole place was...clean.

"I made this place livable," he said, coming around the corner of the suite's small kitchen with a dish towel draped over his shoulder.

"Thanks, Dex. You didn't have to." She gestured around the room.

He shrugged. "Gets me what I want, too, so it's no big deal."

"What's that?"

"Seeing that smile on your face."

Heat crawled over her cheeks, settling on her neck, as she pulled her bottom lip between her teeth. "Oh, yeah?"

"Yep. Which is why I have full intentions of spoiling my wife with the best wrangler gear Boot, Barn and Barrel has to offer. Hell, we'll probably get you a lady Stetson, too."

"I'm pretty sure they just call them Stetsons, dear." She gave that last word the sarcasm it deserved. "And thanks, but I'm fine with my old jeans and a ball cap."

"Nope." He tucked a wet curl behind her ear and planted a kiss on her cheek. "You wanted marriage, you got it."

Oh, boy.

Standing there in front of
that barely hid her rapidly
sure what she wanted an

Dear Reader,

Welcome back to Mercy Hospital! This time, we're heading to an equine-therapy ranch with our hero and heroine, Dex and Millie.

Dex has anxieties about his too-safe life. When his best friend, Millie, retires from an army medic career, they agree to pretend to be married to take trauma therapist positions advertised for a couple only.

Putting the characters outdoors as they delve into their pasts, work past childhood wounds and come together in deeper friendship—and *love*—is reminiscent of my own youth. Nature cures so much of what ails us and I loved playing with that theme in a medical setting.

I hope you enjoy Dex and Millie's love story as much as I did writing it! There's forced proximity, one bed, fake dating and, of course, *friends to lovers*. Many aspects of true love—trust, laughter, intimacy—have their roots in friendship.

I'm excited to hear what you think about Dex and Millie's decision to take their friendship to a romantic level, especially when they're faking being already married!

Drop me a line and let me know what you think on Twitter, Instagram or Facebook, or by email at kristinelynnauthor@gmail.com.

As always, thanks so much for reading!

XO,

Kristine

THEIR SIX-MONTH MARRIAGE RUSE

KRISTINE LYNN

MEDICAL ROMANCE

Harlequin®
MEDICAL
ROMANCE

Recycling programs for this product may not exist in your area.

ISBN-13: 978-1-335-94254-8

Their Six-Month Marriage Ruse

Copyright © 2024 by Kristine Lynn

Harlequin Enterprises ULC
22 Adelaide St. West, 41st Floor
Toronto, Ontario M5H 4E3, Canada
www.Harlequin.com

Printed in U.S.A.

Hopelessly addicted to espresso and HEAs, **Kristine Lynn** pens high-stakes romances in the wee morning hours before teaching writing at an Oregon college. Luckily, the stakes there aren't as dire. When she's not grading, writing or searching for the perfect vanilla latte, she can be found on the hiking trails behind her home with her daughter and puppy. She'd love to connect on Twitter, Facebook or Instagram.

Books by Kristine Lynn

Harlequin Medical Romance

Brought Together by His Baby
Accidentally Dating His Boss

Visit the Author Profile page at Harlequin.com.

To my DU ladies.

Every good love story includes a friendship like ours.
Keep fighting the good fight.

CHAPTER ONE

DR. DEXTER SHAW hung his stethoscope around his neck and resisted the urge to slam the office door. The silence was suffocating. The cool air blanketing the sterile hallway did nothing to tamper the heat boiling beneath his skin. A tingling sensation crept up his arms and his feet itched.

He knew the signs. The onset of a panic attack if he couldn't breathe this one away.

One, two, three.

He inhaled through his nose and out his mouth and it worked, at least enough to keep the edge off. But it was getting harder to keep them in check.

They're getting more acute. More frequent, too.

Bing. Dexter's pager went off, the vibrations barely breaking through the blanket of worry. He clenched and unclenched his hands but the regular techniques—techniques he'd created to help patients deal with their anxieties—weren't working as well anymore. If Dexter was going to permanently outwit the attacks, something was going to have to change, and fast.

Starting with figuring out how he'd been able to keep them at bay for ten years and why they were back now.

Damn thing was his triggers kept changing. Forget the benign dreams-of-my-dad's-death-from-free-climbing-triggers-my-anxiety onslaughts of his youth. These adult versions were sneaky SOBs, ambushing him when he walked by day care and saw his ex, Kelsey, and her husband with their daughter, Emma. Or pouncing on him when he walked through the antiseptic psych wing on the way to his office.

Fears scratched at the door he'd locked them behind after years of being on the patient end of therapy sessions. They whispered something unexpected, something he'd never considered, not after losing his dad so young, then growing up between foster homes without any stability, any consistency.

Maybe you chose wrong, they hissed when he laid in bed, alone. *Maybe your life is* too *sterile,* too *empty.*

Sterile was safe, and empty meant no surprises, but still...

He'd tried to stave the worries off with something new *and* cautious, first by attempting to play the doting dad to Emma when Kelsey adopted her. Maybe he'd been scared of fatherhood for nothing. Then the baby had gotten sick in day care, her temp skyrocketing for thirty-six hours until Kelsey had her hospitalized.

Turned out that kids were the most dangerous threat of all—at least for someone hoping to avoid as much risk as possible so he'd never feel again the way he felt when he lost his dad—like his world was spinning wildly out of control. So he'd tried again with something slightly safer and without the personal attachment he feared—a proposal for a trauma psych program at Mercy—but the hospital's board couldn't find a suitable team to staff it with, so it was on hold.

"Dammit," he swore. "I need to get my act together." A nurse in gray scrubs—one of his staff—gave Dexter a wide berth.

"Yeah, yeah. I'm supposed to be the one in charge, not the one having a breakdown, I get it," he grumbled under his breath.

He groaned into his hands, leaning against the wall of Mercy Hospital's clinically immaculate psych wing. It was his fault—all of it. The problem was he'd willingly cultivated the life that fed his feelings of obscurity, making way for something more serious.

From the moment he'd left the inner-city hospital—a building that had been torn down for a wellness spa since—after almost dying from exposure at eighteen, he'd been a man possessed. He'd sprinted through his twenty-year plan—one designed to leave his tumultuous childhood in the distant past once and for all—and made every single choice that led him to where he was today.

He'd broken up with Kelsey when he realized he couldn't be a dad—not without worrying every minute of every day for the rest of his life. Besides, what could he offer a child when he'd had such a crappy upbringing?

He'd taken the chief of psychiatry position at Mercy instead of the trauma psychologist gig at whatever remote horse ranch Kelsey found that helped first responders work through their PTSD.

The chief job had provided the stability he not so secretly craved after a lifetime without it, whereas the horse ranch would have been temporary, in an unfamiliar environment, and—since the job had called for a committed couple to fill the two vacant positions—it had been too dependent on Kelsey.

It wasn't that he was completely immune to the desire for connection with another person, but a wife? No way. No spouse meant no encumbrances, no one to slip between him and his armor. It meant he could simply work and help patients—the one constant in his life.

Bottom line? He was no victim of his circumstances. *He'd* made every choice that haunted him.

The question was what was he going to do about it now that those choices no longer served him and, by proxy, his patients?

His phone rang, loud and obtrusive in the empty corridor, more difficult to ignore than his discreet pager. But his scowl dissipated when he saw the name on the caller ID. Some of the tightness in his chest loosened as he answered it, and he shoved through the double doors toward the employee parking lot.

"Well, look what the army dragged back. Sergeant Tyler, as I live and breathe."

"That's Staff Sergeant Tyler to you. Reporting for duty."

"Damn. Congrats. I didn't know if or when I'd hear from you. This is a nice surprise."

After talking to his best friend every week for

fifteen years, he'd missed Tyler. This was the longest they'd gone without talking.

"Don't get all sentimental on me now, Shaw. Just wanted to let you know I'm back in town."

"I'm glad to hear your voice. It's been a minute."

"A year and a half. Got held up with the trauma center over there. Would you believe the government pulled their portion of the funding in January?"

"My surprise is overwhelming," he said, keeping his voice monotone and robotic. Sergeant Tyler laughed.

"We got it back, but it took forever to get the center up and running."

"I'm proud of you. Most medics would've quit. Anyway, welcome back. I know some folks that are gonna be happy to hear you're safe."

"Hold the welcome parade for now. Not sure how long I'm sticking around."

"Really? But you just got home. How long till the army yanks you back?"

The silence on the other end was punctuated by the crunch of Dexter's oxfords on the gravel parking lot.

When the hell is this renovation gonna be done so I can stop wrecking my shoes on this shit?

"I'm not going back."

Dexter stopped, the dust he'd kicked up settling on the brown leather of his shoes.

"What do you mean, you're not going back? You're a career army medic."

"I was." Dexter could picture Tyler's furrowed

brows on the other end. "Now I'll be some kind of other career doctor."

"What happened?"

"Nothing out of the ordinary. Job's getting stale." Dex smiled at that one. Tyler was impossible to pin down. The opposite of him, in almost every way possible.

"What else?" Dexter knew his best friend better than anyone. Tyler wasn't being honest.

"I'm lonely," Tyler whispered. If Dex hadn't been standing parade-still, he'd have missed it.

"Oh." Of all the responses, he hadn't expected that. "I thought you'd finally found a solid group of friends."

"I did. They were like family, but they're... they're moving on with their own actual families, starting to put down roots."

"And you want to do the same?" Hope barricaded the fears from earlier. If he could convince Tyler to come back to where it was safe, maybe he'd sleep better at night.

"Not exactly." Dexter recalled the time Tyler had come home with a swollen eye and sliced arm from shrapnel. Dexter had begged Tyler to leave then, before the injuries were more severe. Or worse still, Dex, as Tyler's emergency contact, was delivered the remains of his best friend in a plastic bag. "But I'll fill you in later."

He understood. Tyler might crave the adventure Dex avoided at all costs, but they both wanted the same thing deep down—something that was theirs, something no one could take from them.

Maybe his best friend could find that a little closer to home. "Well, I'm sorry it went down like that. I know how much you liked the people, the travel and hell—even the danger." He raked a hand over his chin, stubble pricking his palm. He'd keep his mouth shut about how relieved he was that Tyler was getting out of a life of risky trauma work, no matter the reason.

"You're the only one who understands that. Thanks for listening. Anyway, I didn't call just to complain. I wanted to know if our Freedom Fridays still stood. I could use a drink."

"Hell yes. But I'm buying."

"Of course you are. Same place, same time?"

Dexter smiled. He and Tyler did these "Freedom Fridays"—the freedom to say anything without judgment—every week Tyler was in the States. The tradition had been going on since Dexter had hit a telephone pole one night after a long shift and without Tyler's lightning quick army medic reflexes, he would have died. A grisly burned-in-his-car death.

Dex offered to take Tyler out for a drink to say thanks when he was out of the hospital—that and to say he owed Tyler one. One drink had turned into them closing the bar followed by a decade and a half–long friendship.

Suffice it to say, Dexter needed that drink, too— and the friendship that had gotten him through some shit.

Death. Deployments…

Panic attacks for mundane nonsense?

"Yep. Maniac MacGee's at six?"

"You done with work by then?"

Dexter's laugh was more a humorless bark. "Whether or not I am, I'm outta there."

His admission was met with a dry laugh. "Wow. I've never known you to leave before the cleaning staff forcibly removes you so they can empty your trash."

Dexter kicked at a small pebble in the shape of a heart.

"Things are changing for us both, sounds like."

"Sounds like we need to tell Mac to keep 'em coming. You have anything tomorrow you need to be sober for?"

Dexter cringed.

Just figuring out what to do about my life and these panic attacks that have been cropping up the past year.

He had a sneaking suspicion it might include leaving a decade-long career at a hospital that had shaped his time as a psychiatric trauma specialist.

"Nah. I'm good." Tomorrow was a lot of drinks away and he wasn't on call. Hopefully the liquid clarity would help him make some tough decisions. Because as he thought of Mercy, of its austere white walls and tranquility, of Kelsey and Liam, her husband and new Mercy trauma doctor, walking through the halls and pointing out his own failures as a boyfriend and father, the painful truth settled in his chest.

He needed to leave. And sooner rather than later.

"Okay, then. Fair warning, I'm gonna talk your

ear off once I have one drink. My tolerance is shit these days."

"Noted and acknowledged. All I hear is you're cheap, so that works for me."

The laugh from the other end was laced with a gravity Dexter wasn't used to. A shiver ran down his spine, tickling senses he'd honed in his profession.

Sergeant Tyler was in trouble, which made Dexter's problems seem like dodging mosquito bites during a firefight. His anxiety—and the panic seizing his chest every third day—would have to wait.

Millie smiled, letting the cool air wash over her. There wasn't a lot in her life worth smiling about, but the spring breeze was a welcome change. She'd lived in surface-of-the-sun heat the past year.

Her smile deepened when she caught the orange neon glow missing the "Gee's" so the sign read "Maniac Mac." That tracked. Mac—her friend from boot camp—hadn't made it past his first deployment when he decided the medical field, especially one in which bombs were being hurled at him while he triaged patients, wasn't for him. He'd quit after his first enlistment and opened Maniac MacGee's, a bar frequented by service members and first responders.

Good thing, too. If it weren't for this watering hole, Millie wouldn't have gotten through the past decade. Her hands trembled as she opened the door, but the shrill twang of a steel guitar worked on her like no therapy could.

She smiled and tossed her unruly curls over her shoulders.

"Well, *holy shit*. I didn't think I'd see your militant ass in here again."

"Mac, you wouldn't know militant if it shot you in the ass."

"Listen, I'll have you know my commanding officer said I had the best IV placement out of any medical recruit if I just—"

"Didn't get that damned case of sciatica," Millie finished.

Mac scowled. "Will you quit bein' mean and come give me a hug? I missed you but making fun of my *medically documented realities*," Mac whined as Millie mouthed the same words along with him, "is no way to treat the man who's gonna be feeding you drinks all night."

"Good point." Millie walked over to the serving window and reached through, embracing Mac. It felt good, holding something solid when her insides felt like they were flapping in the wind. "It's good to see you, Mac."

He squeezed her tight enough to pull the breath from her. "You, too, kid."

"You're three months older than me, Mac."

"Yep. And as your elder, I demand you take a shot to gain entrance into this fine establishment."

"Fine. Whiskey. And not your cheap shit. As the outranking officer here, I'm also gonna demand you join me."

"If you insist."

Mac made a poor attempt at a salute, then poured them each a shot.

"Yikes. That had some teeth," Millie hissed when hers was down, the slow burn of the liquor waking her up like a shot of espresso. "I'll take another, but with a dram of water this time. No need to rush this buzz, it'll come all on its own tonight."

"That bad, huh?"

Millie shrugged as Mac placed three fingers of whiskey in a rocks glass in front of her. Only one person would understand the loss she felt at willingly saying goodbye to a family she'd built, anyway.

"Yep. Hey, uh, not that I'm not glad to see you, but is he here?"

"You know, if you were at all my type, I'd be pissed you're abandoning me for another guy."

She shrugged again, a crooked smile on her lips.

"Sorry, Mac."

Mac nodded to the back, to the booth that had kicked off the friendship all those years ago. "Back there. Here, bring him this," he said, putting another whiskey on the mahogany bar. "I'm not a cocktail waitress."

Millie climbed atop the barstool, leaned over and placed a kiss on Mac's cheek.

"You're the best. I owe you one, Mac."

"I'd settle for an introduction to that man you were in a picture with on Facebook. The hottie in camo. Not everyone can pull off that look, you know."

"Sure thing." Millie laughed as she walked toward the back of the bar, which was shrouded in shadow. Mac had the same taste she did—tortured men with their own abandonment issues.

When she rounded the post at the edge of the dance floor, she halted in her steps. A smile spread across her cheeks at the same time heat built behind her eyes.

"Dex," she whispered. He couldn't hear her— she was still too far away—but he rose and strode over to her, holding a bouquet of purple daisies that were crushed when he wrapped her in his arms and cradled her head against his chest. The dam holding back a torrent of hot salt water broke and her tears fell.

"Damn, Tyler, you're gonna give a guy a complex if he hugs you and you start sobbing."

She choked out a laugh on the edge of a sob and he chuckled, his thick barrel chest vibrating beneath her cheek.

"Okay, okay. No more teasing." He stroked her hair. When his lips pressed against the wild curls, her breathing slowed along with her tears.

Millie pulled back, wiping her damp cheeks with the back of her hand.

"It's good to see you, Dex. You look…*strong*." She didn't let her eyes wander down his frame, which had filled out with hard-earned muscle since she'd last seen him. But her expertly trained touch—a lifesaver when she performed surgery— came in handy. "Been working out?"

He nodded, his shoulder muscles taut. No more runner's body for this guy. He was a brunette Thor now. Like she needed another reason to ignore his pull on her heart.

"Got some stuff to work through and running doesn't do the job by itself anymore. I need to throw a little weight around."

She appraised him through wary eyes.

"Will you settle for sixteen-ounce curls? Because we've got work to do tonight," she said.

His smile broke through. "Hell yes, we do." Dex nodded to the second drink in her hand. "That for me?"

She gave it to him, sipping her own as she sat in the booth. "Mac sends his love."

"Good man. Hey, cheers to you being back in the States. It's really freaking good to see you, Millie." She bristled under the use of her first name. It didn't rub her the wrong way, just made her skin tingle. He'd called her "Tyler" as long as she'd known him. It kept a distance that felt…safer with Dex.

Until… The way his gaze dipped to the deep vee of her light blue blouse added stomach flipping to the mix. *Great.*

He just hasn't seen you in a while and you're different, too.

Millie had always been on the curvier side of the army's regulations, but she'd been doing runs of her own to exorcize the demons that had followed her since childhood. She was still tall and full figured, but with some tone now.

"So, what's been going on with you? Because you look—"

"Like hell?" he finished for her.

"Maybe. A little. Just tired, I guess." That was only partially true. While he did look exhausted, the circles under his eyes textbook markers of sleeplessness, he also looked pretty damn fine. The auburn scruff dappling his cheeks and jaw didn't hurt, nor did the gentle Clark Kent wave in his espresso-colored hair that had grown out since she'd last seen him.

When had he gotten so handsome?

Please. You've always thought he was hot. Do not shove your neuroses on your best friend, her subconscious warned.

It wasn't wrong—she did have a propensity for falling for the wrong guy. Usually that was purposeful; scratching an itch didn't mean the guys had to buy her dinner or anything. It just meant she got what she wanted and could count on not being disappointed when they turned out to be something other than they advertised.

Dex was different. She'd turned him down once—a long time ago, when she was a different younger woman who somehow knew the man whose life she'd saved would mean more to her than just a casual hookup. What that might mean had scared her to death.

Unfortunately, what it had actually meant was she'd guaranteed he only thought of her as a friend since.

So, she'd gone back to casual relationships with emotionally unavailable guys instead of crushing on the one man she couldn't have. Thank goodness, since she'd gotten a best friend out of the deal.

She didn't regret the route she'd forced them down but from time to time, especially as she healed from her childhood baggage, she wondered…

What would it have been like to say *yes* to Dexter Shaw?

Either way, he was off-limits now.

"It's nice being here. Feels familiar," he said. "Remember the first time?"

"Like I could forget. You still had bandages on your head like you escaped a psych ward."

He chuckled.

"This place has heard some shit, that's for sure."

"No joke," she said.

She might have saved his life the day he'd slammed into her life via the pole on Hollywood Boulevard, but he'd been her white knight ever since. Who else could have brought her back to herself after her stepmom—a textbook narcissist—had turned Millie's dad's death into a reason to stop parenting the stepchild she'd never wanted in the first place?

Millie had raised herself from age twelve until Dex came along, the night he got in an accident.

Yeah, he's great, but don't forget he's high maintenance, too, her heart chimed in.

That's an understatement.

While she'd be fine with a toothbrush and running shoes for a week, Dex wasn't his best self unless there was a full-service spa within a hundred-meter radius. That was part of the reason they'd promised, after he asked her out that first week of knowing each other and she shot him down, not to ruin their friendship with a hookup.

They were night-and-day different and what they had was so much more important.

So, yeah. Ignoring the way his looks affected her decision-making was the new standard operating procedure.

"Well, anyway, you're not wrong. I feel like hell. They're back, Millie."

"The panic attacks?"

"Yeah. And worse. They're happening at work now, too."

"Crap. You can't have that." She reached out and took his hand in hers. The familiar warmth that settled between them was punctuated by small bursts of something...*warmer*. With more energy.

"Nope. Not when I'm the literal expert at that place for kicking anxiety and depression."

"What're you doing about it?"

Another shrug. "The usual. Breathing, counting, working out."

"You considered treatment?"

"Long term?"

She nodded.

"I dunno. I've been there and it helped, but... I've been thinking about some other ideas."

"Like?"

Dex shrugged and she tilted her head. "Did you get the trauma team going? That idea sounded right up your alley."

"No, and that's part of it."

"What else?" she asked.

Millie leaned back against the bar and gestured that he continue.

"It seems ridiculous with everything you're dealing with."

"Nope," Millie said, shaking her head. "If I were your patient spouting the same nonsense, you'd tell me not to compare traumas. It's hard for you right now. Period."

"That's fair. Well," he said, running his hands through his hair, "I'm thinking about quitting."

"Your job?" Millie sat up straighter. Damn. That threw a wrench in her plans for the evening.

"Yeah. It might not be the source of the anxiety, but being there isn't helping; I'm sure about that much."

"Can't you step down as chief and just practice?" She bit the corner of her lip. Everything she knew about her best friend said the job was perfect for him—it was safe, consistent and as reliable as a Swiss train.

Selfishly, she needed that to still be true.

Dexter shook his head and only then did she notice the dappled gray hair above his ears, the depth of the lines around his eyes. He looked more than tired. He looked *done*.

"It's not that simple."

"What's Kels have to say about all this?" She'd called out her big guns with that one. Millie knew Kelsey wanted kids, marriage and the whole she-bang. She also knew Dexter didn't.

"We're through."

"I've heard that before," Millie said, snorting.

"No, this time it's for good. She adopted a baby and then the dad came looking for the kid and, well, they fell in love. It was a whole thing."

Millie felt the warm bar air settle in her gaping mouth.

"A *baby*? She fell in love with someone else? What the—"

"You missed a little bit while you were gone."

"Apparently."

He filled her in on a story that sounded like a made-for-TV movie. When he was done, they sipped in silence for a while, the weight of Dex's story heavy on Millie's mind. A tiny voice broke through the fog.

He's single.

She silenced it with an admonition. *It doesn't matter. Only helping him through this does.*

"How about you, Tyler?" Dexter asked when their glasses were more ice than liquid. The return to her last name was jarring. She kind of liked the way "Millie" rolled off his tongue. "I've been patient and unloaded all my trauma at your feet. Your turn."

It was always that easy with them.

She took the last sip of her whiskey, relishing the chilled liquid that still managed to warm her from the inside.

"Well, I'm guessing now isn't a good time to ask you for a job."

CHAPTER TWO

"A—A *JOB*?" Dexter sputtered.

He spit out a half-melted piece of ice. In the background, the lead singer of the band Mac had hired belted a country tune that sounded as heartbreaking as the mood at Dex and Millie's table. A few battle-worn regulars sat at the bar, heads bent over whatever medicinal cocktails Mac had drummed up to cure them of their woes that evening. It was an odd juxtaposition against the three couples slow dancing in the middle of the worn hardwood floor, love—or at least alcohol-induced desire—wafting off them like cheap cologne.

Then there was the woman in front of him, who'd shocked him silent. Just when he thought the stuff out of Millie's mouth wasn't ever going to surprise him again.

"A job? Why do you need a job?"

"You didn't hear me when I said I'm not going back?" She leaned back in the booth, her long brown curls tucked over one shoulder, leaving the other one exposed. He licked his lips in spite of himself. In spite of their fifteen-year-old friendship.

The carnal side of him had to admit—Millie Tyler had grown up. And only gotten more gorgeous in the past year and a half.

But that didn't change the fact that she was abso-freaking-lutely off-limits. Or that what she was asking for was off the table, too.

"If I'm being honest, I didn't think you were serious. You've said it before, Tyler."

"Yeah, when I thought that a job could stand in for my screwed-up family. This—the realization that I've been kidding myself—is different."

Her *voice* was different. Softer. Filled with more than badassery and wit.

"Wow. I didn't know you'd been struggling with them again, Tyler. I mean, your family."

"It's not just that. I was getting restless, anyway. Besides, you're all I need." She blew him a kiss, but the frown lines gave her true emotions away. He stopped short of telling her that putting her happiness in any one person—even her best friend—wasn't healthy. She knew. Besides, he wasn't exactly the paragon of health himself at the moment.

God, he wished he could offer something—anything—that might help them both.

"And if I'm not able to get you a job?"

"Why wouldn't you be able to?"

"Just humor me. What then?"

"Well, if I don't find something here, I'll pick up a DWB contract. They're hiring for the round that will head out in six months. If I hurry, I can get my application in."

Dex's fingertips tingled. Doctors Without Borders was a good gig—one most docs coveted—but it wasn't much less dangerous than a field army medic's job.

"There's really nothing else?" he tried. "Nothing...calmer?" He couldn't lose her to another risky career. Not when he had a chance to keep her here, with him. But at what cost? He wasn't staying—*couldn't* stay—at Mercy. At least not without a leave of absence to make sure he was in the right headspace to treat his patients.

But you have the chance to save her. Like you couldn't save your dad.

"I could go back home to Missouri. At least my stepmom's in a home now."

"Yikes," Dex offered, scoffing at the idea. "That's a nonstarter, isn't it? I mean, she still resents you for leaving in the first place."

"Yup. She still thinks my duty is to her instead of my patients or sanity, despite kicking me out when I was sixteen. Which is why I came to my dear friend Dex with connections at a hospital."

She sipped at her drink and he willed himself to not stare at the way she licked her lips after putting down her glass. Sexy but *dangerous*. Two words he'd always secretly used to describe his best friend when he needed reminders of why they'd stayed just friends all these years.

"Yeah, connections." His voice sounded far away, like it was being funneled from the other side of town.

"So you'll do it? Reach out to your chief medical officer and get me a job? Maybe with me there, it'll save two lives with one set of AED paddles, or however the saying goes. I can help you."

"I dunno—"

"C'mon, Dex. I'm double California Board–certified in psych and trauma emergency medicine, used to long hours and I have great bedside manner. You can vouch for me."

Dexter sighed, the desperation in her voice palpable like the layer of vape smoke hovering over the smoking area on the patio behind them. "It isn't that simple. I know all that and yeah, I can get you the job—hell, I can probably get you *my* job. And if you could find three more trauma docs that are double board-certified, you can take over the program I proposed. But I meant it when I said I was done. I've got no love left for LA, Millie. I need a change as much as you do. This is crappy timing, is all."

She pulled her bottom lip between her teeth. Usually that was a sign she was happy, but tonight it came with weight that knocked him on his ass. He had to adjust his jeans to accommodate the way his body was reacting to her.

Knock it off. She's the same person who slapped you when you tried to hold her hand the night you started Freedom Fridays at Mac's. The same woman who can drink you under the table and still shoot your balls off from fifty yards if you annoy her. But in a sexier package than ever before.

He shook his head, dissolving the battle between his head and…another, less trustworthy, organ.

"Please," she whispered. "I never ask you for anything, Dex. Don't make me beg. Not now." Dexter groaned and put his head in his hands. He'd never had the power to deny his best friend anything, but this was an impossible ask. It was her mental health or his.

"I won't. If you want the job, it's yours. I just won't be there by the time the ink on your contract dries."

"You know that's the important part to me, right? That I'd love you there while I figure my crap out?"

"I do."

"And you aren't gonna make me bring up the fact that you're all I have, are you? You're my family, Dex. You're literally it."

Dexter waved his empty glass in the air in Mac's direction. Their friend nodded and grabbed the bottle and two fresh glasses.

"Oh, thank God," he grumbled when Mac left the bottle and glasses on the table. "Reinforcements."

"Be nice to each other, guys," Mac warned.

"What're you looking at me for?" Dexter asked Mac's back as he walked away. Dex poured them each a full glass of whiskey and slumped back against the hard wood seat. To Millie, he simply said, "I'm sorry. I don't know what to tell you."

"If I'm working with you, I can help you manage the stress," she pleaded. "We make a good team. I'm sure that'll apply to work, too." He tried not to notice the way her bottom lip quivered. An urge to kiss it almost overwhelmed him.

Quit lusting after your best friend. Be there for her.

"Mercy isn't an option for me, Millie. It just… isn't. For a lot of reasons. What good would I be to you if I stayed and fell apart when you need me to be strong for you?"

Millie sat up straighter, her chest out and shoulders back. God, she could have been a general, the way she commanded attention. "Okay, I didn't want to do this, but I'm calling in my favor."

Dexter stared at her, his pulse quickening while his brain slowed. "You wouldn't. Not now, Millie."

The stare she shot back intonated all the seriousness of a three-alarm trauma. "Why not? It's not a favor if you don't have to give something up for the other person. I know what I'm asking is impossible, but you told me I could use it for anything. I saved your life and you owe me." She sat back and downed the rest of the liquid in her glass, hissing after slamming the glass on the wood table. "So, I'm using it for this."

"Whether or not you saved my life remains to be seen," he muttered. "You should've left me in the Porsche that night. Would have done us both a favor."

"Uh-uh. Nope. We're way too far down the line to start up that pity party. Dex, if you can't help me, I'm gone. I'll take the DWB job, but it's not what I really want."

Dex groaned. She was handing him what he'd wanted for so long—his best friend close by, safe and in a stable, permanent job. But taking that gift would be to shut out all the change he knew he needed to get his own life on track.

But then an idea hit him. She just needed a job.

Frankly, so did he. But they didn't need to be at Mercy... Did they?

Part of his current anxiety stemmed from over-correcting when it came to creating a life of safety. *So, what if...* What if he did something totally out of character and tried something *new*? They could apply somewhere as a team—a small clinic somewhere, or even a rural hospital. If it didn't work, he could always leave after the usual six-month probationary contracts most places offered.

And he could take a leave of absence at Mercy so he didn't cut that tie completely. It wasn't like he didn't have the PTO after a decade of slight workaholic tendencies.

Hope surged in his chest, pushing back the fear that had taken up residence as of late. He leaned across the table, regretting it immediately when the dim bar lighting illuminated gold flecks in Millie's green eyes. He could get lost there, no doubt. But she'd shut that down a million years ago, which meant he'd best honor her choice.

Not that they were similar enough to make a go of it, anyway. And he'd never treat her like a one-night stand. Never. She was too important.

"What if I could get you a job with me, but not at Mercy?" He studied her reaction, the way her eyes focused, growing wider even as her lips twisted in scrutiny.

"Like where? I'm not working at a drive-through, Dex. Not that there's anything wrong with that, but I still want to help people. I'm a doctor and I don't want to give that up."

"Me, too, Millie."

"So, why would you leave the job you're in? You're established at Mercy. And I know damn well you aren't going to follow me to a gig where there's less than top-notch amenities available."

He tilted his head in thought. Because what she said was true. He'd love to travel with Millie, seek out a new adventure, but he'd done enough adventuring and restarting for a lifetime. He could use a change, but she'd called him on a fundamental truth of his—he needed a sure thing in a safe place. The opposite of what Millie wanted.

He swallowed a groan.

"I dunno. Maybe we can take a road trip and check out places we're interested in."

She snorted. "We travel well together, I agree, but *you*? In a car for who knows how long? Yeah, no thanks."

Dexter tried to keep his face passive, but after three shots of hundred-proof liquor, that was getting more difficult. "Excuse me. What's that supposed to mean?"

"You're a diva."

"Am not."

"Are, too. Remember Italy?"

He sighed. "Are you always going to throw that in my face? It was *Europe*. You're supposed to be fashionable."

"Were we supposed to wear different clothes to each meal?"

Dexter drained his glass. "See if I ever buy you a welcome-home trip again."

"All's I'm saying is I don't think that's the answer. I'm not against looking for a new place to land together, but it'd be better if you could use the connections you've made over the years if we're going to find something outside LA. Then we're not shooting in the dark."

"I wish I had any. That was Kelsey's MO, not mine." He looked down at his drink, wishing it had the answers.

"Hmm. Well, calling her is off the table, huh?"

"Uh, yeah." Dexter didn't like the sarcastic snort that escaped his throat. "Besides, the only connection she had that would have related to us and not obstetrics was at a ranch for wounded vets. It was some trauma psych job that used horses and other ranch-related stuff to treat PTSD in veterans and first responders."

"Equine therapy."

"Yeah, I think that's what she called it."

Millie sat up straight. The twinkle in her eyes was all too familiar to Dexter. It was the same glimmer that had led to the two of them at the top of the tallest peak in Arizona one autumn night. The same one she'd had right before she convinced Dexter to try skydiving in Temecula.

It was mischief and resolve and the signal that he'd already lost whatever argument she was going to make.

"Let's do it. That's *perfect*, Dex. I mean, working with horses? It'll do us both good and think of who we'll be working with—the same patients we always wished we could focus on. Weren't you trying to start a trauma psych program at Mercy?"

"Yeah, that part's true, but the rest?"

Safety. Security. Consistency.

None of those things existed at the equine ranch.

"I don't ride horses, I don't like to be dirty and I don't own a set of cowboy boots. You said it yourself—I'm a diva. It won't work. Besides, it was for a married couple."

Checkmate. Gin. Yahtzee.

He let the smug grin spread across his face.

"And?"

He took a long sip of whiskey, feeling fidgety again. He shifted on the bench. "And we're not married, Millie."

"Neither were you and Kelsey."

"True. Kelsey and I were gonna fib a little for the sake of the job, but we were at least *dating*."

Millie leaned forward, the look in her eyes steely and determined. His smile fell.

"Tell me she knew you half as well as I know you."

"She didn't. Obviously. And in the end, I realized I didn't really know her, either."

"Exactly."

"So, what does that have to do with us?"

"I can pretend to be your wife."

Dexter choked for the second time that evening, this time on the alcohol. It burned along the length of his throat.

"You can do *what*?"

Millie smiled in a crooked half grin that said

he wasn't going to like what came next. She stood up and motioned that he scoot over to let her in his side of the booth. He did and regret followed swiftly. Forget the gold in her eyes... Her scent—something floral and feminine—snaked around his throat, suffocating him.

He...*liked it*. Liked it on *her*, even though anything floral or feminine was diametrically opposed to the fierce army trauma medic he knew.

"I'll be your wife. Do you need my credentials for that, too?"

"Oh, no, Millie. I—"

"As long as you do the cooking, I can take care of the rest," she continued. "I work all day so I won't nag when you have to, I don't mind keeping the place clean and—" she paused and sent him a little wink "—I'm a freaking maniac in the bedroom."

Dexter swallowed hard. He did *not* need to know that.

She licked her lips. "And outside the bedroom if that's more your taste."

Dexter shook his tingling hands and damn if his jeans weren't a little too tight around the waist.

"Even if I agreed to this asinine plan—which I'm not," he added when her eyes got as big as her smile, "it'd be a fake marriage. Sex wouldn't... It wouldn't be part of it."

His whole body sagged under the pathetic statement.

"Why not?"

"Because you're my best friend." His tongue was suddenly too thick in his mouth.

"I didn't mean the sex, silly, though I'll add that's your loss. I meant why won't you consider the plan?"

"Besides the fact that it's not a plan?"

"It is, too. Are they still hiring?"

"As far as I know." He'd overheard Kelsey saying the couple that had taken it when she passed it over was done with their contract and she wished her and Liam could take the job, if only they could bring their daughter.

"Great. Call them up, tell them you'll take the gig, and send our credentials."

"Fine. Let's say we did that. There's a million other reasons this still wouldn't work," he added so the topic could move away from things that were sounding more appealing with Millie by the minute. Like how the body he'd known most of his adult life might feel pressed against his.

"Oh, yeah? Like what? Your lack of horse awareness? So what? You'll pick that up."

"Maybe," he hedged. Though the thought of being around the smelly animals day in and out wasn't exactly appealing. That was part of why he'd turned down the offer the first time. "But there's also the fact that no one will believe *we're* married."

She scowled, the look somehow endearing.

Just friends. You're just friends.

"Excuse me, Dexter Shaw, but why not?" He cringed at the hurt in her voice. "Are you saying I outkicked my coverage with you?"

"Not at all." He rubbed his eyes with the heels

of his palms. Where was Mac when he needed the guy? The idea that Millie wasn't good enough for him was laughable. If anything, it was the other way around. What did he have to offer a woman of the world—a stunning one at that—with his stale, safe life? "I'm saying you want to travel and have an adventurous spirit and I...don't."

"And?" Why did he get the sense she was winning this whole argument with that one word?

"And our lifestyles don't fit. You belong with some mountain man who chops his own Christmas trees and hunts everything he eats. Someone who'll bring you wildflowers from his expeditions."

"I'm more of a beach gal," she teased, picking up a pretzel from the bowl on the table and popping it in her mouth. "Especially after Trevor."

"Yeah, he was a tool. But at least he lived within a hundred miles of you. And I agree—you belong with some long-haired hippy who plays the acoustic guitar by a bonfire and can sweep you off your bare sand-covered feet."

"That sounds like heaven. Just so you know, I'm picturing Jason Momoa with a ukulele, though." A small twinge of jealousy pricked Dex's skin. He shook it off. "But I get what you mean. You'd fit more with some charity do-gooder with coiffed blond hair and a closet full of suits. Like Kelsey, or that other girl you dated who wore makeup to the gym."

"Bev." He'd made it a whole month with the aerobics instructor before he was bored stiff. And that was saying something.

"Ha! Yeah, her."

Millie was right—that was more his taste. Someone safe, planned. Not someone who flitted through adventures like she was in a Bond film.

Not someone like Millie.

"Okay, but this would only be a six-month gig. What happens after that?"

"I apply to DWB," she said, shrugging in her usual nonchalant way. "And you're off the hook."

Why didn't *off the hook* sound as appealing as it should? Especially when she would be off doing God knew what with Doctors Without Borders. An urge to take care of her, protect her, almost choked him.

"Do you have to do work that's so dangerous?" he asked.

"It's not like I have a choice. You took LA off the table, so what's left? Besides, someone has to." Millie pulled her hair back off her face and tied it up with a band from her wrist. Though he'd always appreciated the wild curls that framed her face, he couldn't keep his gaze from the curve where her slender neck met her shoulder.

"Still."

"You know," she continued, "one might argue that living without the trappings of a life of luxury makes me free."

"I'm sure someone might. You, on the other hand, know better because you know why I'm like that, Millie. I'll tackle my issues, too. I'm just asking—as a friend, and your best one at that—that you consider not always throwing yourself into such threatening situations."

"We'll talk about that later. Unless you want me to apply to DWB right now, I'd say we have other things that need our attention. Like this equine doctor job."

She clapped her hands and the smile she wore resembled a kid who got a pony for Christmas. He chuckled, realizing that if they took this job, she would actually get a whole barn of horses for the holiday.

"But what if the job actually isn't available? What then?" It was his last attempt to stave off the inevitable.

Millie dug around in her purse and Dexter took the moment her back was to him to appreciate the sculpting of her shoulders, the curve of her waist. She turned around as he was mid lip-lick and he cringed. Great. It only took fifteen years for her to catch him looking like a creep.

"If you like what you see, we can always put sex back on the table. Literally." She winked and handed him her phone while he tried to find his voice. That had to be the whiskey talking, right? Because they'd already crossed that bridge and decided to stay in the neutral zone where only friendship was allowed. "Here. Call them."

"Seriously?"

"Serious as an effing aneurysm. We both need the job, and really, what other options are there? I'm also willing to bet that whatever trauma recovery program we'll be running will do us both some good."

Dexter couldn't disagree with that. In fact, the only thing he could disagree with was pretending to be Millie's husband. Not because he didn't know more about her than anyone on Earth, or because it wasn't plausible that the two could be together, but because...*it could.*

He'd watched her walk into the bar, slide up to Mac and own the place with her confidence and, if he were being totally honest, her knockout looks. She'd always been pretty, but she'd become captivating since the last time he saw her.

His head hurt trying to come up with a way to convince her this was by far her worst idea yet. Hopefully the headache and sobriety that greeted her in the morning would do what he didn't have the guts to do.

"If we do this, I'll need to take some time off to get my head right. I can't dive right into something else until I know I'm good to take on new patients."

"That would be good for me, too, to be honest."

"And if they don't want to wait, then I can't entertain it, Millie."

She nodded and put her drink up to her lips, draining it. "Nope. I understand."

She licked her lips, and between that and the mischievous gleam in her eye, Dex didn't have a chance.

"Okay," he blurted out. "Let's give it the ol' college try."

Millie squealed and leaned over, planting a kiss

at the corner of his lips. "Thank you! You won't regret this, Dex. I promise."

She wrapped one arm around him and used the other to fill their drinks.

Oh, I think I just might.

CHAPTER THREE

Two months later

MILLIE HAD NURSED her hangover for two days after that night at Mac's. Her head had pounded from the multiple tumblers of whiskey she'd thought was a good idea at the time, but that was nothing compared to the way her pulse raced every time she thought about the lie facing her down. It was almost two full months later and she still couldn't calm her racing heart when she thought about it.

Christ, she thought for the thousandth time since she'd received the one-line text.

We're in.

What have I gotten myself into?
In less than a week, she'd be Dexter's *wife*. Not really, obviously, but for the six-month provisional contract, that'd be her secondary role after trauma physician and psychologist. Which meant she and Dex would have to sell the lie every damn day, since the contract had them living on site in a small one-bedroom cabin.

Millie paced in the small hotel room she'd rented now that she was back in LA.

Two months.

Two months had passed and she'd barely spoken to the guy since Mac's. He'd been serious about taking a leave of absence, checking himself into some fancy wellness spa where every sip of water was probably flavored and the thread count on the sheets didn't dip below four digits.

She'd crossed her fingers and wished on every damn yellow light that he found the clarity he needed in his wellness sessions to stay at Mercy, where they could work side by side but stay just friends.

No dice. He'd sent another one-liner the day prior.

Out. Looking forward to catching up, cowgirl. See you soon.

Ugh.
Soon sounded like another four-letter word.

At least she'd had two months to get in some of her own therapy sessions, which were honestly something she should have done years earlier.

Except they hadn't prepared her for having a *husband.*

Millie grabbed her running shoes. She'd call Dex that afternoon to make a plan, but not until she ran out her feelings—feelings a therapist couldn't touch. Tying her shoes and throwing on a running hat over un-showered curls, Millie replayed their last non-text conversation from the morning after Mac's.

"You sure this is what you want? That working on this ranch for half a year and pretending to be married to me is gonna help you fill the hole in your life? Because I can get you a spot at my retreat and we can look at other options," he'd said the next morning. She'd seen the "get out of jail free" card for what it was, but some mix of pride and negative thought indicators had prevented her from speaking up.

"Yup," was all she managed to squeak out, to almost immediate regret.

Dex.

As my fake husband.

Dex, who'd tried to hold her hand out of pity after a few too many drinks that first night he took her out to thank her for saving his life.

As my fake husband.

Dex, who she turned down because he was too good a guy to lure in with her "charms."

As my fake husband.

Not exactly living the life she expected of her patients, was she?

Someone knocked on her door just as she got to it, water bottle in hand. A glance around her sparsely decorated hotel room said room service couldn't have come at a better time.

Take-out containers from every region and ethnicity littered the surface of the desk-slash-table. Scattered tissues left evidence of a *Bridget Jones* level of self-pity, dotting the paper and plastic containers. Then there was *her*.

A glance in the mirror confirmed it—she'd seen better days. Her hair looked capable of housing a small family of sparrows, hat or not. Her cheeks could land planes with the moisture dappling her pale skin, and her eyes… Well, racoons would be jealous of the circles she'd developed. She'd never been as ritualistically clean as Dex—only a select few people were—but this was bad, even for her.

"Ugh," she said, slapping her cheeks to give them some color. "Get a grip."

She whipped open the door and blanched.

"Dex," she croaked. "What are you doing here?"

He glanced over her shoulder at the self-loathing bomb that had exploded behind her.

"I could ask you the same thing."

She attempted to tuck the nest on top of her head farther under her running cap, but only an exorcism and prescription-strength moisturizing conditioner were fixing that mess.

"I'm…um… I'm relaxing a little before we start." Didn't she deserve a couple days of bingeing Netflix and eating takeout after leaving her old career behind?

Dexter pushed his way into her room, and as if her mortification knew no limits, he sniffed the air and his amused smile twisted like he'd inhaled antiseptic-masked defecation in a patient's room.

"A few days to relax is a jaunt to Telluride or a weekend getaway to Catalina Island. This is a cry for help."

She sniffled, another round of "my life, a dry comedy of errors" pushing at the back of her sinuses.

"I know."

The admission seemed to buy her an ounce of

empathy. Dexter pulled her into a hug and kissed the top of her head.

"I'm sorry, Millie. You've been through hell and I all but left you the past two months."

"You texted," she said, her voice muffled by his strong chest against her cheek.

"Well, I'm not going anywhere again. Being present is what good husbands are supposed to do, at least according to the blog I read this morning."

She pulled back and looked up at him.

Big mistake.

His blue-gray eyes were the only things on earth capable of cracking through her carefully constructed armor.

"You read a blog?"

"Turns out a thirty-eight-year-old man who's never been married isn't exactly an expert in the field of faking what marriage should look like. So yeah, I may have opened a tab or two in the name of research."

She smiled, the chink in her nerves letting in a thin swathe of light. Maybe this wouldn't be so bad, after all.

"Did you forget the part about me knowing you better than anyone? I'm pretty sure your apartment looks like my hotel room if you swapped the fast food with clinical psych books on healthy relationships."

He smiled, too, and the light grew brighter.

"Elliot Aronson and his theories on cognitive dissonance send their best."

"Are you saying this thing we're doing doesn't mean we're certifiable?"

"He'd argue that, so sure. Let's go with it. Anyway," he said. "We can't do a thing while you look like that."

He gestured to the whole of her and the heat of mortification flashed up her neck.

While she appreciated the solid strength of his chest propping her up, she was also painfully aware what that strength mixed with his scent was doing to her. Whatever pine tree wrapped in coffee grounds he'd rubbed up against made her want to simultaneously climb him limb by limb and run her tongue over his body in the same way.

Not a good way to start a *fake* marriage.

"I was going running."

"Sure you were." He walked her toward the bathroom instead of the hotel room door. "Okay, here we are," Dexter declared, depositing her in front of the shower. "You can be lonely, but you can't be lonely *and* smelly while you're out with me."

"Out with you where?" Fear dappled her skin. "I'm not ready for public consumption yet."

Dexter clicked his tongue and winked. "I know, which is why we're shopping. To get ready."

Maybe it was the wink or the sodium in her veins from too much takeout, but her knees buckled. He caught her under the arms. If Dex wasn't... *Dex*, it would have been romantic, being held in the arms of the man she cared most about.

"Why do we have to shop? I have plenty of clothes." He steadied her again, but the weakness in her body remained. She really could use that run to get her head and heart rate right.

"You're making me take a job on a *ranch*. In case you weren't aware, there are animals the size of trucks there, and they don't care if my loafers are genuine Italian leather. We're shopping so we can survive in Cambria."

He turned on the water and went to lift her arms, but that shame she wouldn't recover from.

"I've got it from here, Dex."

He rested a hand under her elbow, and though he'd seen her in all stages of undress and vulnerability over the course of their friendship, this felt the most intimate. His gaze bore into hers and a chill raced over her exposed skin.

"Hey. I'm just worried about you." That was Dex, through and through. He always worried about her choices, her adventures, her one-night stands, even though they were just friends.

Not anymore. Now she was his friend-slash-wife.

"I'm fine. My therapist might have been off a dark alley with a threadbare couch instead of in Malibu with cucumber water, but she was good. I've got this."

"We can joke all day long and it won't change the fact that your family left you high and dry— both families. You're allowed to feel things, Millie."

He'd dropped the *Tyler* altogether. With a job that required them to manifest a five-year-long marriage starting in just days, that was probably a good thing. But she could use a little distance right now.

"Thanks," she finally said. "I'm glad you're here."

"Me, too." He opened the cheap plastic shower curtain and all but shoved her in. "Okay. No more stalling. Get in before the stench of three-day-old Thai food sends me into my own ward of the hospital."

Millie obeyed, grateful for the stinging heat of the water that pulsed over her skin. She felt better under the hot spray. Under Dex's care, too.

Half an hour later, a brush easily slipped through her hair and, more importantly, Millie didn't feel the thick heat at the back of her throat anymore. Wrapping a towel around her chest, she poked her head out to see what Dex was up to.

"What did you do?" she asked. The whole place was…clean. Not even the corner of a soy sauce packet was left behind.

"I made this place livable," he said, coming around the corner of the suite's small kitchen with a dish towel draped over his shoulder. Despite his efforts not to, he looked domestic. It suited him, despite his persistent disagreement about the merits of domesticity. "You're welcome."

"Thanks, Dex. You didn't have to." She gestured around the room.

He shrugged. "Gets me what I want, too, so it's no big deal."

"What's that?"

"Seeing that smile on your face."

Heat crawled over her cheeks, settling on her neck, as she pulled her bottom lip between her teeth.

"Oh, yeah?"

"Yep. Which is why I have full intentions of spoiling my wife with the best wrangler gear Boot, Barn, and Barrel has to offer. Hell, we'll probably get you a lady Stetson, too."

"I'm pretty sure they just call them Stetsons, *dear*." She gave that last word the sarcasm it deserved. "And thanks, but I'm fine with my old jeans and a ball cap."

"Nope." He tucked a wet curl behind her ear and planted a kiss on her cheek. "You wanted marriage, you got it."

Oh, boy.

Standing there in front of Dexter, clad only in a towel that barely hid her rapidly beating heart, she wasn't sure what she wanted anymore. Only that if she looked too deeply into that question, she wasn't sure she'd like the answer.

CHAPTER FOUR

DEXTER SWALLOWED A Millie-in-tight-jeans-induced lump back into his stomach where it belonged. You'd think after two months of prepping to come to Cambria—including deciding how best to sell their fake marriage—he'd feel more prepared, but that wasn't the case. Besides the lie, neither of them had worked with horses, or even been on a ranch, so there sure as heck wasn't anything he should find alluring, except…

"This is hideous."

Not the word he'd choose to describe her, but like hell he was gonna say what was really on his mind.

"You look—"

Sexy? Gorgeous?

"Dexter Shaw, if you know what's good for you, you won't finish that sentence. I'm an expert marksman in three combat rifles and two handguns."

"Duly noted." He tipped his Stetson in her direction, trying to loosen the tightening in his chest. "But fitting in will be half the battle in getting the patients to trust us as their doctors."

She scratched under her hat, her pink lips twisted into a tight scowl. It wasn't so much that the light green flannel he'd purchased—along with the matching boots and hat that yeah, were a bit much—brought out her eyes. It was also the way the jeans hugged curves he'd never let himself check out.

"Whatever you say, *honey*," Millie grumbled. She twisted the gold band on her left hand until he grabbed both her hands and squeezed.

"It's going to be okay."

"I know," she shot back. She wriggled out of his grasp and opened the door to the cab. "Seriously? You don't have a ladder to go with this thing?"

"The salesperson said—"

"It was the best they had to offer, right? Jesus, Dex. You're nothing if not consistent." They'd bought a truck—or rather, *he* had, with the substantial savings he'd accumulated before taking this leave of absence from Mercy—and he had to admit, cowgirl outfit notwithstanding, she looked good riding next to him.

If only she wasn't ready to tan his hide, or whatever cowboys called it. Millie was pissed.

Pissed is better than lonely and sad.

Besides, as adorable as she looked angry with him? Yeah, not a good reason to stop teasing her.

"Wait there, wifey."

Dexter hopped out of the truck, sprinted over to Millie and carried her out of the truck.

"What are you doing?" she hissed.

"What I didn't get to do since we eloped," he said, alluding to their cover story. "Carrying you over a threshold."

She glared at him from under the wide brim of her hat.

"Dexter Shaw, you are skating on thin ice."

"You wanted this life, and you've got it. Let's try and make the most of it."

"That's pretty uncharacteristically optimistic of you, Dex." Her gaze raked over him and it got a few degrees hotter under his flannel.

She's right, his subconscious demanded. *You're happier.*

Maybe it was being around Millie, the one person he didn't have to hide from, or the way the country air in Cambria moved freely in and out of his lungs. Or even the eight-week stint working on himself before they left the city. But he felt... lighter. No hints of the inky black tendrils pulling at his thoughts, closing his throat with fear.

"Okey dokey. And if I forget to thank you later, I really am grateful that you're doing this," she said. "This outfit is ridiculous, but I'm actually...excited about something for the first time since I enlisted out of high school."

He took her hand and walked down the long dirt driveway to the barn where they'd been told to meet. Risking one of the weapons Millie was so proficient in being trained on him, he bent down and kissed her cheek.

He appreciated the bloom of pink that spread across her cheeks.

"Me, too. All right, it's go time. Ready to be Mrs. Shaw for the next six months?"

She nodded right away, but he saw the way her throat struggled to swallow. He understood. This was a big lie to keep up. If it were anyone other than his best friend on the other end of it, he'd have canceled the whole thing.

Dexter pushed open the heavy oak door, the creak in the hinges exactly what he'd imagined when he thought of this moment. In fact, every inch of what they walked in on was par for his expectations.

Dust they kicked up lingered a few inches off the ground, clinging to every surface in the barn—the doors, the walls, even the ceiling was coated in it. The only two exceptions were the riding equipment hanging on the stall doors—*tack*, if he remembered right—and the horses themselves. They were both shiny and clean. Interesting.

"Wow," Millie whispered. "This is just what I imagined."

Dexter smiled at the synchronicity. "Me, too." It was always that easy with her.

Just like that, his smile fell, though. He couldn't let himself slip into an alternate reality where he and Millie were *actually* together.

Why not?

Dexter lifted the hat from his head, desperate to let what little breeze there was in. No time for that line of thinking. He might have worked out his recent anxiety issues, but Millie's penchant for danger would ramp them back up if he were her actual spouse.

And risking their friendship when their differences inevitably clashed? A nonstarter.

"Well, howdy," a deep, booming voice called out behind them. Dexter spun around and was hit with a wave of embarrassment. The man walking toward them was every inch the cowboy. Tall, strong like he'd been lifting the horses out of their stalls, and wearing a Stetson that didn't look like it was bought yesterday.

The only thing not "cowboy" about the guy was his simple black T-shirt and worn pair of loose-fitting jeans. No flannel chambray, no butt-huggers as Millie called them. Dex glanced down at his own outfit and realized Boot, Barn, and Barrel had duped them.

"I'm Gale Brooks, the owner of this outfit. You must be the Shaws."

He extended a hand to each of them, a steely gaze to go with it.

"That's Tyler-Shaw for me. I'm a hyphenate." She smiled up at Gale, whose crooked smile said he liked her spunk. Or was it just that he liked *her*?

She's married, buddy. Eyes off.

Hmm. Where'd that jealousy spring from?

"I'm Dr. Dexter Shaw, and this is my wife, Millie."

The words rolled off his tongue easy enough, but the ripple back into the cavity of his chest was severe. *My wife.*

"Dexter Shaw… You shoulda been born into ranching with a name like that."

Millie grinned like she'd won a prize. "He doesn't like horses."

Dex shot her a scowl. "I like them fine. I just haven't seen the need to be on the back of one in the city."

"We'll take care of that. Riding isn't required, but it'll help you bond with your patients to get them out on the trails between individual and group therapy sessions."

"I can't wait," Millie added. To Dex, she whispered, "That'll teach you to dress me in flannel."

His jaw set. "You forget, married couples get divorced all the time, dear," he whispered back.

Gale clapped and gestured to the fields and main ranch house visible in the distance. "Well, okay, then, Tyler-Shaws. Welcome to Hearts and Horses Ranch. We're not your typical roping-and-cattle-riding ranch, though we are fully operational."

"I read on the website you hire vets and first responders who've gone through the treatment program to work the ranch," Millie said. She did? Research was usually *his* forte and she just showed up ready to go along for the ride.

"That's true. Every person here is either a United States veteran, like myself, or a retired first responder, like my partner." Gale tipped his hat to Millie. "Corporal Brooks, ma'am."

"Staff Sergeant Tyler—" she started, then glanced at Dex "—Tyler-*Shaw* reporting for duty."

Dex exhaled. They needed to corroborate and practice their backstories more seriously if they were going to pull this off. Slipups like that were gonna get them found out.

"And lemme just ask. Your paperwork didn't mention you served in the military, fire department, or police force, Mr. Shaw. That correct?"

"It is." Why did he feel like that was a shortcoming all of a sudden?

"No worries. It's not required for the physicians on contract. I just want to know how to introduce you to the patients."

"Dr. Shaw is fine."

"All right, then. I'll show you to your bunk, then you can meet the clients at dinner. Just so you know, we all pitch in around here, outside our general duties. Since y'all are just settling in, I won't hold you to dinner duty, but come breakfast, it's all hands on deck."

"Sounds good," Millie said. "We're excited to start."

Speak for yourself, Dex thought. They walked back to the truck, Gale insistent that part of the welcome package included his assistance with their bags.

"After that," he said, "you're on your own."

Gale hefted the first of Dex's oversized suitcases out of the bed of the truck like it was filled with goose feathers. "You're lucky you drove. I don't think a plane could take off with this bag," he said, smiling at Millie in a way that made Dexter uncomfortable. There was friendly and then more than friendly. This was the latter.

"That's my bag," she deadpanned, pointing to the carry-on sitting on the tailgate.

The cowboy laughed. "Well, I'll be. Don't know I've ever met a wife who packed less than her husband."

Millie gestured back to Dexter, who had to repress an urge to defend his masculinity. "This guy plans for all possible scenarios. I just brought jeans and a few tops. Hope that's okay."

"You've got the right idea. All's you need out here is a comfortable pair of boots for work and a cleaner pair of the same thing for hitting the town on your nights off."

Gale took both heavy bags over his shoulders. Millie carried her own, leaving Dex empty-handed.

"I can get those," Dex said.

"No problem, son. I'm used to carrying more than this, though you're testing that limit," he teased.

"I've got medical supplies packed in there, too."

"So do I." Millie grinned, clearly not helping his case for overpacking.

"You know, for all the teasing you do, you're forgetting the time you had to use one of my button-downs as a dress when your luggage was lost on that Vegas trip," Dexter whispered to Millie. "My overpacking has saved your ass once or twice."

"Maybe. But that was only 'cause I didn't have *anything*. You, on the other hand, could have opened up a Brooks Brothers."

"You two sound like you've been married longer than five years," Gale laughed.

"We've been together fifteen," they said in unison.

"Feels like more than that," Dexter grumbled under his breath.

It was clear, then. Of all the jobs he'd had in life—therapist, chief of psychiatry, even being a medical transcriptionist in college—being Millie Tyler's husband was gonna be the toughest gig of all.

Millie whistled while she changed. It was quiet out here—no gunfire, no shouting. But also no laughter from her army medic bunkmates, no teasing from her nurse, Sarah, about her crummy card-playing skills, no one to read her like a book when she got quiet imagining the ghosts of her past.

Just the distant sounds of cowboys doing whatever cowboys did. She didn't hate it; fake-marrying Dex notwithstanding, this seemed like a good move. But after being alone most of her teen years, then filling the void with chatter from work the next decade and a half, the quiet would take some getting used to, for sure.

One thing was certain—she hadn't breathed this easy since, well, maybe ever.

Dex jumped in the shower after unpacking, citing "dust in every damn crevice" so she had the room to herself for a moment. It'd been obvious why the ranching doc job called for a married couple when they saw the bunkhouse. Theirs was the only "suite" and even then, it consisted only of a full-sized bed, a shower with a clear curtain and a toilet that—*thank the gods*—was tucked away behind a door that closed and locked.

No kitchen, no office. *No privacy.*

Dex hummed a country song from her high school years. George Strait, if she remembered right. At one point, he launched into the lyrics and she froze, listening intently.

The man can sing.

Of course he could. Aside from his penchant for the finer things, he was perfect. Not exactly *fake* husband material.

The shower turned off and Millie sprinted through putting lotion on her legs. It might be dusty, but it was also dry as the desert she'd left mere weeks ago.

"Hey, have you seen my—" Dex said, coming around the corner from the tub. He stopped at the corner of the bed and before he caught himself, she saw his gaze travel across her stomach and bare legs before landing at her feet. It gave her the split second she needed to give him a once-over without letting him in on just how gorgeous she found him.

Clad only in a towel—and a small one at that— water dappled his skin and wet hair hung across his eyes. But his chest and shoulders... The strength complemented the emotional, sensitive man she knew. Which she very much appreciated.

"What are you doing?" she asked, grabbing an off-white T-shirt and throwing it over her nude lace bra. Dex had the good sense not to say anything, but the heat that flashed on his cheeks said it all. She'd embarrassed him on day one. *Great.*

"Showering. What are *you* doing?"

"Changing. There's no damn way I'm showing up to meet a group of rugged patients in creased jeans and a green flannel. I don't know why I let you talk me into getting that shirt in the first place."

Dex smiled and her guard lowered just enough to let the grin past her defenses.

"C'mon. You looked adorable."

"Yeah, just the professional impression I was hoping to make."

Millie watched, horrified, as Dex combed his hair, dug through his queen-bed-sized suitcase and brushed his teeth—all in a towel small enough to make a Victoria's Secret model blush.

She fought to look away, but she was only so strong and Dex was…tempting enough to test that strength.

"Okay," he said ten minutes later when—thankfully—he came out of the bathroom in jeans and a loose-fitting shirt. "So we can both agree those outfits I bought were a fail. Luckily, I overpacked," he said, shooting her a pointed look, "or I wouldn't have any replacements."

"Yeah, real lucky you brought—" she lifted a white button-down shirt off the top of his garment bag "—a *white* shirt you have to iron after you wash it. To a *ranch*. We don't have an iron or bleach strong enough to get the country out of this if you stain it."

She grinned until his gaze dipped to the bigger of his two suitcases.

"You didn't," she laughed.

"It's just in case. I wasn't planning on using it."

"Sure. You brought an iron *just in case*. Dex, you're always good for a laugh, that's for sure. We should head out, though, unless you need to shine your oxfords or something."

"Knock it off. Hey, before we leave, you wanna talk about the sleeping arrangements?"

"What arrangements? There's one bed."

"Yeah, but we're not—" he lowered his voice as if he didn't want the cows mooing off in the distance to hear him "—actually married."

"I know," she whispered back, conspiratorially. "I was there when we agreed to it."

His glare was adorably overdone, like the rest of the man. Good grief, she was gonna have to hold his hand through this thing, wasn't she?

"Well," she continued in normal volume, "you packed pj's in that clothes coffin, didn't you? We'll be fine."

"Pj's? What are you, ten? I'll have you know the only things I wear to bed are a plan for tomorrow and a smile."

Her body froze cell by cell despite the heat. "You're kidding."

"I'm not. How didn't you know that about me? Remember Vegas when you got in my bed by mistake?"

She didn't. The amount of vodka sodas she'd consumed that night could have floated the Titanic back to the surface. She wasn't sure whether it was a bad thing she didn't recall a naked Dex or a miracle she'd give thanks for later. As it was, she had the image of his Greek god physique in a tea towel seared into her retinas.

"Whatever. I'm an adult, you're an adult, and we'll just manage. It's only six months." Her brain did the math without prompting.

One hundred and eighty-some days. Good luck, sister.

"I'm good if you're good."

"I'm good." This trip, this job, this place—none of it was so that she could jump her best friend and satisfy fifteen years of curiosity and longing. It was to help patients like her start their own healing process.

Her heart beat to the tune Dex had sung in the shower.

Shut up, she told it.

Maybe his wouldn't be the only hand she'd have to hold as they navigated their new circumstances.

"Okay. Now that the sleeping stuff is handled, should we get to work?" she asked.

"Yep. Let me just get my cell."

"Why bother? We won't have service out here, anyway."

Dex's twisted lips and furrowed brows said this was going to be a long six months for him, too.

"No cell. No nice clothes. No iron. You have no idea how much you owe me for this, Tyler. And a night of drinks ain't gonna cut it."

She smiled, but the *Tyler* dug at her heart. They could fake being in love to the outside world as much as they wanted, but behind closed doors, they were still Shaw and Tyler, best buds who kept their hands to themselves.

For a split second, she played the what-if game with the day she met Dex—something she did when things were tough, or the wanting of him threatened to override her promise to stay friends.

In a different life, the man who'd slammed into Hollywood Boulevard right in front of her bistro table where she'd been on a shitty first date would have been strong, capable and, yeah, a little bit of a diva. The same as the man she knew and cared for today. But if she could choose? She would have been open to more, to the possibility that, regardless of the crappy short hookups she'd had in the past, *they* could be more. However, thanks to the wreckage from her past *situationships*, all she pictured back then was the morning after when she'd have said goodbye to Dex like all the rest and then where would she be? Without a helluva good man that she was lucky to count as her only family.

Maybe in a different life.

When they shut the door behind them, Millie waited for Dex to fix his boots. She inhaled deeply, the scent of pine laced with a hint of salty sea air.

"I keep forgetting Cambria is close to the water. Maybe we'll get a day off and can head to the beach sometime."

"Sure," Dex mumbled. "Who doesn't love sand in all their skin folds?"

Along the tree line, something moved. Millie trained her gaze and saw a deer and her baby emerge. They weren't hesitant here—they must feel safe from predators on the ranch. She inhaled deep and let that resonate.

"Is there anything you actually like about this place?" she asked when Dex stood up.

"The shower's got good water pressure."

"Wow. High praise," Millie said, snorting.

"It's just not my cup of tea. It'll be fine, though. We're here to practice medicine. I don't need to fall in love with it or anything."

"Maybe. But all this fresh air, the songs and sounds of the wildlife—this place will grow on us and I'll bet my salary you won't even want to go back to LA when this is done."

She went to toss him a wink and smile and instead found herself wrapped in his arms, his gaze hot and pinned to hers. His lips were only half a breath from hers until...they weren't.

When his mouth crashed into hers, heat flashed across her skin along with confusion.

What the—? her brain tried, but her heart silenced it.

Shut up. We're kissing Dexter Shaw.

Millie let his tongue tease open her lips just enough that she tasted the mint from his toothpaste. She moaned as her body relaxed into his. His arms tightened around her, his strength the only thing keeping her knees from buckling.

This. This is what we've been missing just being this guy's friend.

When his hand tunneled into the base of her curls, her stomach flipped in response.

And then, with the same unexpectedness of being kissed in the first place, it was over and Millie was standing there—*where*, she couldn't be sure of anymore—alone and wanting.

"I'm happy to be here with you, hun."

Hun? She was still dizzy from the kiss. Maybe she misheard him?

"Uh…me, too, Dex." Her fingers traced where his lips had just been. That simple five-second time lapse had shifted everything she thought she knew. All she comprehended was wanting more. Like, *now.* "That was nice. I mean, do you want to talk about—"

"Okay. We're clear. Whew. That was close."

"Clear? Close?" Millie's head spun to catch up to her racing heart.

"Gale was watching us from the barn, and I just wanted to show him how in love with each other we are so he doesn't get suspicious. I think that did the trick."

"Yeah. I'll bet it did." Disappointment settled in the crack that had opened up in her chest during the kiss. *Of course* it was fake. Their whole relationship, aside from being best friends, was fake, so why would that earth-shattering kiss be any different?

Maybe she'd gotten it all wrong; maybe Dex would find faking it with her easy because he didn't have any real feelings for her. Maybe she was the one in trouble because she couldn't separate the physical longing for him from the show they were putting on.

"Anyway, what were you saying? Oh, yeah, how this place would grow on me?" His smile was so clueless, so genuine, it hurt to see. "I think you might be right, Tyler. I already feel better."

He strode off toward the barn and she sighed. This gig might do wonders for her medical career, for finally putting her crummy childhood behind her, but her heart was going to end up an unforeseen casualty.

CHAPTER FIVE

DEX SAT ACROSS from Millie on the wooden bench, careful not to let their feet touch under the table. Not that it mattered. His whole body had been buzzing with electricity since he'd kissed her.

What the hell were you thinking?

As bright ideas went, that wasn't his smartest. The thing was it'd made sense to him to dip in and kiss her since Gale's face was scrunched up like he'd stepped in something. Dex had reasoned that getting found out would be worse than playing a game of lip-lock with Millie, who he'd explain himself to after.

But…*whoa!*

The aftereffects of the kiss weren't something he anticipated, nor could he shrug them off. He swallowed and pulled at the neck of his soft cotton T-shirt that seemed too tight all of a sudden.

Everything came into sharp focus for a second.

The refurbished barn looked chic enough to host a wedding, with string lights, pale blue tablecloths and mountains of food. The massive pine table was filled with good home cooking—thick palm-sized biscuits sat in a basket in front of him, their warm buttery scent tickling his nose; monstrous slabs of pot roast smothered in onions and a brown gravy vied for attention next to the basket. There was even a salad and what looked like a berry cobbler farther down the table.

But he didn't have a damn bit of appetite. For food, at least. He glanced at Millie, her head tipped back mid-laugh, the bare skin of her neck glistening under the barn lights.

Could she distinguish what they'd have to do to keep from getting caught from the truth—that they were just friends? Or was he the only one who all of a sudden couldn't figure out what was real and what wasn't?

"You're the doc from LA, right?" a voice on his left asked.

Reluctantly, Dex pulled his gaze from Millie, a near-impossible feat since her bottom lip was pulled between her teeth as she listened intently to a police captain tell his story of finding Hearts and Horses.

"Um…yeah. Dexter Shaw, nice to meet you."

"Ray Warren. Nice to meet you," the man said. "You just get here?"

"Yep. Arrived this afternoon. It's a nice place."

"Sure is. It's my fourth year and I still don't get sick of the fresh air, the morning rides."

"Wow," Dex said, sneaking a sideways glance at Millie. Were her eyes always so bright when she talked? "Four years, huh? You must find it pretty therapeutic."

"You could say that. I'm actually one of the staff now. I did two summers here as a patient and now it's my second as a stable manager."

"I'll have to pick your brain about how to get on the good side of those half-ton beasts we saw in there earlier. I know my way around a trauma bay or hospital, but this is like Mars."

"You bet. We'll start tomorrow. You mind handing me that bowl of potatoes?"

Ray's smile was wide, his hair long. But when Dex's gaze dipped for a fraction of a second, he saw limp fabric where a right arm should be and metal protruding from beneath his shorts on the same side. "I'd grab 'em myself, but..."

"Of course." Dex handed Ray the potatoes and tried not to look at his injuries.

"It's okay to ask. I'm used to it by now and that's why we're all here, to heal from what ails us, right?"

Did that include missing limbs? Dex had worked with critically wounded patients before, but few inside the walls of Mercy.

"A bomb?" Dex asked.

"Gas explosion after a fire in an office warehouse we responded to." Ray pointed to his shirt, which read I Had a Blast Working for Redondo Beach Fire Department in black letters against a red-and-yellow explosion.

Dex couldn't help but chuckle at Ray's sense of humor, but the weight of what he and Millie were going to face sat heavy on his chest. Would she be able to work with these folks after her own traumatic experiences as a child and in the military?

He risked another glance at her, but she was smiling, the small gap between her front teeth showing. It looked good on her—damn good—but more than that, she was smiling despite talking to a young man with a burn scar running the whole length of the right side of his face. Her chest rose and fell evenly and a glance at her hands showed them steady and calm.

She was okay, it seemed. *Good*. But the last thing he wanted was to be the weakest link with her on a personal *and* professional front. He needed to get his head right, put aside the feelings from the kiss—likely just a hormonal reaction after too long without physical affection.

"Damn. I'm sorry," Dex said, focusing back on Ray. "You still ride?"

"Why not? I'm not gonna let a couple measly limbs keep me from doing what I love. Besides, that handsome man over there wouldn't let me live it down if I gave in to these injuries and stopped living." Ray nodded to Gale at the end of the table.

"Is he your…?" Dex trailed off.

"Boyfriend? He doesn't put titles on things, but we've been living together for two years now, so he'd better start."

Ray laughed and scooped a heaping serving of potatoes on his plate before sliding the bowl back to Dex, who added some to his plate as well.

They ate in silence while Dex considered all he'd been wrong about in the past few weeks.

Gale, for one. Turns out he hadn't been flirting with Millie earlier that day, and if the smiling patients up and down the table were any indication, he ran a pretty stellar operation.

Which meant Dex might just be wrong about this place, about the possibilities that awaited them.

Then there was the infinitesimal nudge his heart gave his chest when it thought of Kelsey. He didn't want *her* anymore—maybe never had, not fully—but perhaps he wanted what she had in Liam and Emma? A...a *family*?

A couple months ago, the idea would have been unconscionable, but now?

That might still be a stretch, but his reaction to another glance at the group of people swapping stories and dinner plates said more human connection might not be a bad thing.

Look at Millie, the most consistent part of his life and what he'd gotten most upside down. He'd worried about caring for someone else most of his life, thanks to a mom who hit the road before he was old enough to drink from a cup and a dad who'd been solid and wonderful to Dex, except for his penchant for adventures that had ultimately gotten him killed. The aunt who had watched Dex for the short times his dad had been away hadn't been keen on adopting him, so he'd been forced into the rough end of a foster system that wasn't kind to six-year-old boys. All these years later, he straddled two lives—one of solitary existence that posed no risk to his heart but was lonely as hell, and one where he craved what he'd lost when he lost his dad.

Millie was the bridge, the first person he'd trusted since his dad died. She'd shown him that caring for another person wasn't a death sentence, even though she, like his dad, often chose risk and danger over calm and safe.

"Hey, Dex." He looked up and saw at least four

pairs of eyes on him, including Ray's and Millie's. "They wanted to know how you proposed."

At her words, the entire room fell silent as if they'd been waiting for this moment all night. Dex's jaw tightened. They'd rehearsed the story, but he hadn't thought he'd have to deliver his first performance in front of the twenty or so patients and at least a dozen staff.

"I figured since you're the one who popped the question, you'd want to share it." Her grin was wide and her eyes sparkled with mischief.

"That's so sweet of you, *honey*," he said.

"Y'all might not believe it, but this man here is as romantic as they come." She blew him a kiss and Dex swallowed back a snort. Not even *he* believed that. No way they would, especially as the six months wore on and he couldn't act on that lie.

That was one problem he'd always had with wanting a spouse or family—aside from the juxtaposition they created. They demanded to be put first, and with the exception of doing this for Millie, he didn't operate that way. None of his foster families ever taught him how, nor did his time living on the streets when he'd run from the system. He was good at taking care of others when he could follow a clinical procedure, but predicting the needs of someone not under his medical purview?

Impossible.

"Well, where do I start?"

"Start with the flowers you brought."

"Flowers?" he asked. They hadn't discussed flowers.

"Yeah, to the pier." She winked. What game was she playing at, trying to trip him up? Didn't she know what they risked if they were caught? Fraudulently misleading an employer at best.

"Oh, yeah, the pier. Well, I brought pale purple daisies, which are her favorite, but damn hard to find in winter." That much he knew from fifteen years of friendship. Her smile said he'd done okay. But her eyes narrowed in surprise. Did she not expect him to remember? "Luckily Pietro's keeps them in stock year-round."

"They do?" Millie asked. Dex tried not to gloat at the matching incredulity in her voice.

"How else do you think I got them for your homecomings?" Another truth sprinkled amongst the lies. He brought her a bouquet of the rare flowers every time she came home.

"Hmm," she said, her gaze focused and cheeks painted a light pink. "Anyway, go on."

"Yes, please," Ray said, leaning his chin on his hand in rapt attention.

"Well, I brought the flowers and her favorite maple-glazed donut from Donut King since it was the morning of the anniversary of our first official date," Dex continued.

"From when you hit the telephone pole?" Thomas asked.

She'd already told them that?

"Uh, no, the drinks I took her to after I got out of the ICU. We walked along the beach, talking and eating. Then, when we came up to a small crowd at the water's edge, she wanted to see what was going on."

"Tell me there was a ring, maybe a band playing her favorite song," Ray said, his eyes closed and a wide grin on his face.

"Oh, please, Ray," a woman from the other end of the table chimed in. The scar on her cheek was visible from where Dex sat. Maybe he'd call his closest work colleague, Owen, out to consult. He was a genius when it came to reconstructive trauma surgery. "He's the incurable romantic here. Unrealistic, too."

"It's not that unrealistic, actually. There wasn't a band, but Dex did ask a guy from his hospital, Remy, to play his acoustic," Millie said.

Remy was just the kind of guy Dex was always teasing Millie about since he was more her type—long hair, played the guitar, believed in romance... *Him* with Millie the patients would have no problem believing. Too bad that wasn't the story they were selling.

Dex swallowed his insecurities with a sip of tea.

"Am I telling this story, or are you, hun?" He winked, taking a play from Millie's book. Her lip tucked back between her teeth and her cheeks flushed the same color as the vibrant pink sunset that evening. His heart fluttered in his chest and he rubbed the spot absently.

"Go for it," she said.

"Well, between my buddy playing 'Unchained Melody' and the message I'd had a local artist draw in the sand, it didn't take much convincing once I got down on one knee."

The crowd of patients and staff erupted into cheers and questions, which Millie fielded like the expert she was. Even Gale came over for a moment, putting his hand on Ray's shoulder and squeezing it. He kissed the top of Ray's head before heading back to the kitchen, a soft smile on his face.

That was nothing compared to the one on Millie's. Dex had watched her face transform as he shared their fake engagement tale. What began as a teasing smile had turned serious yet warm. She wanted those things—the romance, the wooing. She wanted a great love, even if she wouldn't admit it since every adult in her life since she was a kid had shown her how silly a notion that was. But it wasn't, and he was only keeping it at arm's length from her by pretending to be something he wasn't.

But that kiss...

He shook his head. The kiss was an anomaly, a reaction to someone he cared about deeply, but it wasn't portentous of anything more. They'd promised to stay friends, and even if they hadn't, their differences were far greater than their similarities; they'd drive each other up the wall.

"Ten minutes till the evening group sessions," Gale called out from behind the pony wall separating the kitchen from the open dining space. "Drs. Tyler-Shaw, you're welcome to sit in on this one until tomorrow when you pick up your own sessions."

Thank God.

Dex had never been so happy to go to work.

"Well, that's it, I guess," Millie said, shrugging.

"You guess? It's all incredibly romantic, but don't forget to keep it up now that you're working together. You know that—?"

"Fifty-eight percent of couples who work together end up divorced," Ray said to a patient with an emergency medical technician T-shirt on. "We know, Thomas. Please stop reminding us of dire circumstances and let them be happy. Clearly, they're in love and doing fine. See the way they look at each other."

Dex glanced at Millie, whose chin was lowered. Her eyes met his, though, and the promise they'd made didn't loom as large as before. How *did* they look at each other? He wouldn't know love if it slapped him upside the heart, but he knew he couldn't live without Millie in his life. That wasn't the same thing, though.

You sure about that?

Confusion swirled with the food in his stomach, and he grew queasy.

The last thing he wanted was to send Millie mixed signals, but she knew the gig. This was a part they were playing so neither of them had to go back to jobs that were killing them. That, and so they could help people like them—damaged and slow to trust. If they blew it, more than healing would be broken in the process. Besides, it was six months, then she could chase a real happily-ever-after and he could, well, figure out what he wanted next.

You're sure that's not her? his heart asked.

A whisper of doubt crawled along his skin. His fingers traced the place her lips had been just an hour ago, recalling the very real, very *intense* feelings the kiss had drudged up. The question that sat on his mind, weighing it down, was what it all meant.

Was it the result of a lonely body finally given a chance at affection? Or was it Millie's effect on him? Dex sighed as he got up from the table and gathered a pile of plates to clear. He wasn't sure of anything anymore, it seemed.

Millie nodded, listening intently as Ray shared his story for the trauma group he was leading. The group of firefighters, EMTs, veterans and police officers who shared afterward were from varied walks of life, but all injured in the line of duty. The stories might have been drastically different, but their circumstances weren't—each struggled to regain physical and emotional well-being.

As group therapy went, the setup was pretty standard. They sat in a circle, all of them equal in rank and experience. No one's previous positions were mentioned—just their diagnoses of acute PTSD. Not all of the patients had physical injuries, either. Some of them shared stories of watching everyone around them bleeding out or blown to bits only to walk away with nothing more than survivor's guilt.

But the collective weight of loss in the room was palpable. She and Dex had their work cut out for them if they only had six months with these patients.

"Would you like to share?" Ray asked after everyone had taken a turn. He'd been kind and patient with each of them, explaining what wasn't their fault and thanking them for being brave enough to share with the group. But Millie wasn't ready.

Her skin itched as she plastered on a fake smile and shook her head.

"No, thanks. I'd love to soon, though."

"Of course." Ray closed out the session and the vets broke out of the circle to mingle. The fact that they liked each other enough to bare their souls, then hang around and chat pulled at Millie's chest. She desperately missed the community of her fellow service members.

Would she ever find that sense of family again?

"Hi, Dr. Tyler-Shaw." Millie smiled. She'd been Sergeant, then Staff Sergeant Tyler, but this was the first Dr. Tyler of her civilian career. It sounded good. "I'm Sergeant Banks—third battalion, first squad army ranger. I just wanted to introduce myself since I'll be your first patient on Monday."

"Nice to meet you, Banks." Banks's eyes shifted toward the door, then the window. Millie's heart ached for the man. On the outside, he looked fine—tall, muscular, every bit the soldier. But she recognized the invisible injuries—darting eyes looking for exits, assessing the unforeseen risks around the room, cataloging the escapes… It was classic PTSD. "I'm glad you're here."

"Me, too. I'm looking forward to talking more

to you and your husband. It'll be nice to have his perspective as a civilian."

Her husband.

Dex.

A shiver raced across her skin, which she attributed to the cool mountain air closing in around her. But she couldn't mistake what it meant when her fingers absently traced her lips, recalling the kiss that had seared them.

"I'm looking forward to it, too, Banks. Have a good night." He walked away and Millie caught a slight hitch in his right knee.

"Are you settling in okay?" Ray asked.

"We are, thanks," Millie said. *We?* Why had she roped Dex into it?

"Good to hear. You know, this is a safe space for you to share, too. I know you're the doc, but it'll do them a world of good to know you have your own story."

Millie gulped a grenade-sized lump back into the pit of her stomach.

"I know," she whispered. "And I want to. It's just... I'm not sure how to..."

"How to say it and keep it all together?"

Millie nodded. That was exactly it. Of course, Ray would get it.

"Well, give it time. The sessions will help; even leading them puts my mind right most days. The horses won't hurt, either. There's something about being outside, the ocean air swirling around you, sweeping your problems away while you work with your animal."

"That sounds nice. I'm looking forward to riding, actually. Practicing medicine again, too."

"And then, you can't beat curling up with your sexy man at the end of the day, nothing but the sounds of the hills between you."

Ray winked. Hopefully he didn't notice the heat that traveled up her neck. Of course, she'd pulled her hair back so her skin could showcase every emotion she felt as she felt it. Darn her half-Irish heritage for making it impossible to hide her feelings.

Curling up with Dex.

She licked her lips. In fact, that one thought had plagued her since he let drop the fact that he slept in the buff. Then, of course, he'd gone and kissed her, sending her spiraling and unable to think of much else. Even the delicious-smelling dinner had been an exercise in mechanics only. She couldn't recall a bite—a travesty since that berry cobbler had looked delicious.

"Anyway, I'll leave you to it, but Dr. Tyler-Shaw?"

Millie glanced back at Ray. "Mmm-hmm?"

"I'm mighty glad you're here. Gale did a good thing bringing you two to Hearts and Horses."

All Millie could do was nod, a meaningless gesture she lamented as she walked back to the bunkhouse suite. The attached building housed the rest of the staff and the sounds of a guitar and laughter drifted from the open doorway. Millie ached to head that way, if for no other reason than to avoid going "home" to her fake husband.

Until she glanced at her door.

Dex leaned against the wooden frame, his feet bare and his undershirt untucked. He'd discarded his dress shirt and his hair was tousled. His arms crossed languidly across his chest and he held two bottles of beer by the neck in one hand. When he held one out to her, she took it, appraising him after they clinked bottles and silently pulled at the beverages. The cold liquid should have been unwelcome, given the way the night had sucked the heat from the desert air, but the warmth wafting off Dex was enough to counter the chill.

"You look relaxed," she commented.

"I feel relaxed. I know I gave you grief earlier, but this is growing on me."

"Me, too."

They sipped in silence, and when he lifted an arm, she took the unspoken invitation and leaned against him. His solid frame held her upright like it had dozens of times over the course of their friendship. But this was the first time she felt like she could open up about what she wanted in the darkest hours of her nights. Things like her desire for a family and life that looked relatively boring on the outside.

Planting gardens instead of traipsing through vast desert wastelands.

A good man to love and cherish instead of sleeping with the worst of them to sate a physical ache without the guilt of using someone.

A career spent near her life at home.

At one point, Gale and Ray walked by them toward their cabin, Ray's arm draped around his boyfriend's. The couples nodded at each other and Millie's heart clenched. On the outside, she and Dex looked every bit the married couple in love. They knew everything about each other, joked and were tender in equal measure, and even physically showed affection like an actual couple.

But one problem stuck out to her as she filled Dex in on her group therapy session instead of the hidden treasure trove of secrets she held close to her chest.

She was crushing on the wrong man. Optics aside, Dexter Shaw would never want a real marriage and family. The sooner she remembered that, the less painful being his wife would be.

CHAPTER SIX

MILLIE CHANGED HER mind immediately after their teeth were brushed and *her* pajamas were on. This little arrangement they had would never get easier, not when Dex stepped out of his jeans, draped them on the side of the bed, then did the same with his boxer briefs. He stood there in all his fine masculine glory a full three and a half seconds, plugging in his phone, before pulling back the covers and slipping under them.

"Ready for bed, wifey?" he asked, a sly grin on his face.

She nodded, feeling more naked than he was in her baggy T-shirt and pale blue lace underwear. Trying not to stare at how he somehow kept the ridges of his abs when he was sitting, Millie followed and got into bed.

"You're really not going to wear boxers?"

His brows quirked. "I can, if you'd prefer it."

"Um, maybe." She swallowed hard. "I mean, yeah. Would you mind?"

"Of course not." He slid them back on, but it didn't make a damn bit of difference now that she knew what hid beneath the thin fabric. "Good God, this thing is comfortable," he said.

"You say that like you're surprised."

"I dunno. I kinda figured Gale wouldn't spring

for the good stuff when the point is that we're supposed to be roughing it."

"I don't think that's the point, but yeah. I'd never have thought it by looking at this place," she said, gesturing to the sparse room acting as the entirety of their home for the next six months, "but between the food, company and this bed, I'm already happy we left LA."

Dex's crooked smile snuck under the thin defense she'd mustered to avoid staring at him naked. Shoot. The fact that she could still see his smile meant they'd forgotten to turn off the lights.

"Dex, the lights," she said.

"Yep, they're on. My wife—you know, the last one in bed—forgot to turn them off."

She shook her head. "Nope. You promised to love and take care of me for life. That means shutting off the lights before bed so I don't, I dunno, break a toe or something."

"Is that right?"

"That's right."

Dex sighed. "I'd kill for a remote-operated light right about now."

Millie grinned, her hands pressed together in silent pleading. That is, until he threw back the covers and, wouldn't you know it, he hadn't somehow in the past few minutes put more than his boxers back on. Why hadn't they moved to Siberia or Alaska where Dex would be forced into wearing more clothing?

"You know what?" she proclaimed, hopping out of bed in one swift move. "I just happen to love you enough to take this one for the team," she said, more to her heart than to Dex. Because the less she had to watch her desires strut across the room in godlike form, the better.

"Wow. I'll take it."

Millie sent up a tiny prayer of thanks that he pulled the covers back over his body just as she turned out the light. She fumbled back in the pitch-black, feeling in front of her for obstacles. The biggest one, unfortunately, was in bed with her.

"See? No broken toes," Dex teased.

"Um…nope. All good here."

A total lie.

Her heart raced loud and fast enough she worried it could be heard over the whirring of the overhead fan.

"Another thing I miss about LA?"

She couldn't see Dex between the new moon and lack of anything resembling a streetlight, but she felt him inch closer to where she lay still as a body in the morgue.

"What's that?" she whispered. There weren't many, but another bed sounded good right about now.

"Ambient light so I could see you while we talk."

She inhaled a sharp breath when his calf settled against hers. It wasn't unexpected, especially with how tall the guy was, but it sure felt like it right then. He might as well have picked her up, pinned her against the wall and made love to her, the way her leg tingled with awareness.

"I'm actually pretty tired," she said, garnering

a yawn that sounded as fake as their marriage. "Maybe we can chat over breakfast?" She turned her back to him, curling up into as tight and small a ball as she could.

"Sure. Good night, Millie," he said. She flinched. Why did it have to sound so intimate when he used her first name? The flinch turned to a full body freeze when his hand rested against the small of her back. Jesus. He was going to make this as difficult as possible, wasn't he?

He was a *good* guy—and her best friend, at that. But giving into this…*thing* she felt brewing would ruin both. She stared at the place where the blinds met the edge of the window and willed herself to fall asleep.

Despite the inauspicious start to their night, Millie awoke to her alarm, surprised at the time. She must've drifted off immediately, but her body felt heavy, weighed down as if she'd tossed and turned all night.

She stretched—or tried to at least.

Something heavy was literally pinning her down. A glance to her right showed the culprit. Dex's arm was wrapped fully around her, and only then did she notice his body curved against hers.

Oh, God. They were *spooning*.

She gave in for a moment, letting his solid warmth hold her, knowing the moment she moved, he'd shift and the dream would burst open like a summer coastal storm, leaving her shattered against the rocks of reality. When he nuzzled closer, his hips tucked close to her backside and he let a small moan escape as his length—clearly in full morning salute—pressed against her.

Oh. My. God.

If what she felt was any indication, he'd be more than enough to fill and satisfy her. Hell, she already knew they had the chemistry to back it up—their kiss still reverberated hot on her lonely lips.

Dex rocked into her, his breathing still deep. He might be asleep and unaware, but she was wide-awake.

She bolted up, throwing his arm off her in the process. His eyes fluttered awake but he didn't look aware of their previously compromising position.

"Good morning, Millie. Damn, I slept like a dead guy."

"Good morning. Uh…me, too."

"You been up long? I didn't hear you get out of bed."

"No, just a few minutes. But I'm going to head out for a run before we have to start the day. Feel free to go back to bed if you want and I'll wake you up when I'm back."

The run wasn't part of her plan—yoga was, actually—but the cramped space in the room would feel too much like she was posed on display for him. She needed distance.

"Actually, a run sounds good. Mind if I join you?"

She swallowed back the retort sitting at the base of her throat. *No. You can't. You're too much of a distraction.* Calling attention to that would be giving the thought power, and she needed to nip it where and when she could.

"Sure. We leave in five."

She dressed quickly, desperate for the desert-meets-ocean air that Cambria was famous for. Anything to take her mind off her naked best-friend-slash-fake-husband.

Dex's hand brushed against the small of her back. "I'm ready. Shall we?"

"Yeah, follow me. Ray gave me some ideas of which trails to take."

Irritation gathered where his hand once was. She wanted his hand on her back. And on her stomach, cupping her jaw while he kissed her, sliding down the waist of her tights… But she couldn't have it—not all of it, anyway. Not the emotion that came with the caresses.

So she needed to avoid anything that would lead to those emotions.

Millie took off toward the hills behind the ranch, faster than was probably smart, but literally running away from her feelings seemed the only option.

Dex's heavy breaths behind her drove her around the edge of the property and up the steep embankment at its border. The terrain meandered between cactus and tall yellow grass interspersed with thick sea green bushes. It was typical central coast landscape, especially on a ranch, but she wanted what came next. Ray had told her there were ocean and wine country views at the top, but she couldn't look up to see how far that was or she'd stop. She needed to take this step by step.

Think about something else.

Her breathing became labored. A flash of sprinting away from her childhood home with all its broken skin and promises, breathing much as she did now, seared her retinas.

Millie pushed harder.

Who are you most excited to work with?

From a staff perspective, she was excited to work alongside Ray. His expertise may not be in practicing medicine, but it was earned in personal experience. When he completed his master's in psychology, he'd be an asset to the whole field.

Dex's footsteps stumbled, but she didn't glance back. They fell back into step, just a few paces behind her now.

The young woman, Reese. I want to work with her most, I think.

The first responder had a severe limp in her left leg, and from what Millie saw on her way out of the dining hall the night before, scarring around her knee that said she'd barely kept her leg at all.

"Can you hold up a sec?" Dex asked. His question came on the wheezing end of an exhale. "I need to tie these shoes."

She shook her head. She couldn't keep waiting for him.

"I'll see you at the top. I've got to keep moving."

Millie felt his absence behind her as she took short quick steps up the steep rocky trail. It was freeing, but also empty. So much of her life was like that, wasn't it? She made her choices, left behind the toxicity of her family, which was liberating but lonely.

When the terrain evened out, her breathing slowed and she finally allowed herself to look up. Half a breath lodged in her throat and she coughed.

"Damn," she whispered. "Thanks, Ray. This was worth it."

In front of her, the pale yellow light of the early sun painted the edge of the horizon and reflected in fragmented shards across the expanse of deep blue Pacific water. The breeze hummed with salt and life and everything she'd missed about LA's beaches. Behind her, rolling hills draped delicately with dry gold grasses were dotted with bright swathes of green where vines had taken root and found life beneath soil too sparse to keep anything else alive.

She, Dex, the patients at Hearts and Horses— all of them were kind of like a pinot grape vine, resilient and tough enough to make it through the hard times.

Her hands rested on her hips and a tenuous peace settled over her. She'd given up so much—her job as a trauma doc in the army, her military family, her childhood—but she had this, her future. And that was something.

"Good God, woman. You can run, I'll give you that."

Dex stumbled up the edge of the path, out of breath and flushed. He'd shed his cotton T-shirt along the way, tucking it into the back of his shorts like a tail. Millie averted her eyes from the gleaming bare skin of his strong chest, keeping her gaze pinned to the sparkling water below instead.

"Damn," he said, echoing her assessment of the three-hundred-and-sixty-degree views. "This is ridiculous."

Millie nodded. "It's beautiful."

"Worth spending the next six months here?" he asked. He rubbed her shoulder, something he would have done any other time in their friendship. But today, it landed differently. She read meaning into it where there wasn't any. The kiss had been a decoy, the morning cuddling a sleep-induced mistake.

Dex might be able to separate the physicality of their relationship from their emotional one—and maybe at one point, before the fake-wife thing, she could have, too—but she couldn't any longer.

"Yeah," she said, maneuvering out of reach of him. "I'm glad we'll be able to make a difference here."

"Me, too."

They gazed out over the water, the distant sound of gulls the only noise aside from the brisk breeze whipping around them. Millie's skin had begun to cool now that her heart rate had slowed, and she shivered. Dex reached for her as if he meant to rub her arms to keep her warm, but she shook her head.

"Don't," she whispered.

"What's going on, Tyler? What did I do?"

She scoffed at the use of her last name.

"Seriously? Tyler? *That's* what's going on."

"What do you mean? I've always called you—"

"I know. Let's just leave it. We've got breakfast

in forty-five minutes and our first round of patient sessions just after that."

"I'm sorry if I offended you somehow, but I'm just trying to find my way through this thing. This thing *you* asked for, need I remind you."

Millie's arms prickled, not with the chill, but the truth in his words. She gazed over at him, a mistake since the gentle morning light reflected in his eyes along with hurt. Hurt she'd caused.

See? This is what happens when I let my misguided feelings get tangled with a man like Dex. I take his heart of gold and dull it with my own nonsense.

"I'm sorry. It's just—" She shook her head, weighing her options. The truth? Or her friendship? "I didn't sleep well," she offered, going with the latter. No reason to involve him in her inappropriate feelings after all this time.

"No worries. I'm sorry if I kept you awake."

She shrugged off his constant attentiveness, his pervasive need to see her happy and safe when the one thing that might actually work was the one thing he couldn't give her.

"I think I know what might help," she said, trying on a grin.

"What's that?"

She gave one last longing look at the ocean spread in front of her like a bounty. "I'll be back soon," she whispered only loud enough for herself. To Dex, she said, "Race you to the bottom," and took off down the hill without waiting to see if he'd keep up. When it came to him, she'd always be three steps ahead but still finishing last.

Dex listened to Sergeant Dominic's story with rapt interest. The man had been a police detective for eighteen years, lost six friends in the line of duty and was the father of two boys, one of whom needed special care for his autism.

What the hell do I have to complain about? Dex wondered. *My life's been a Lifetime movie compared to this guy's.*

He knew enough to know he shouldn't compare traumas, but still, George Dominic was showing him a perspective he'd not had in a while. Sure, he'd worked with a couple firefighters and EMTs who'd seen or experienced something horrific, but for the most part, his practice dealt with the Hollywood elite and their specific brand of nuanced trauma, most of which was caused by too much money and not enough boundaries.

This was a tough new gig, but far more rewarding.

"Anyway, I don't really know how I found Hearts and Horses, but I'm glad I did. They're already helping me get back to being the kind of man I need to be for my sons. I damn near gave the force everything and now it's time to save what's left for my family."

"That's a great outlook," Dex said, putting his legal pad down and leaning on his knees. "But what're you saving for yourself?"

Dominic's lips twisted in confusion. "What do you mean?"

"I mean, what are you doing in all this caring for other people to fill your own cup?"

"I'm here, aren't I?"

Dex smiled kindly. "You are, and that's going to be a huge step in your recovery. But so is working on something that's just yours, something that your career or your family can't touch."

"Hmm. I never thought about it that way. But my wife has been through so much supporting me in this career that only chipped away at both of us."

"She sounds amazing," Dex said, reverence in his words. "Worth doing right by."

"She is," Dominic agreed. "Can we talk about how to do that next session?"

"You bet," Dex said, walking Dominic out. He thanked the man for his public service and honesty in the session and closed the door behind him.

As Dex poured himself a cup of coffee, his thoughts drifted to Millie, to all she'd been through with no one to support her, no one to help her relax after her own military service and frenetic childhood.

Was he doing right by *her*? Fake husband or not, he was still her best friend, which meant it was his job to keep her safe and look out for her when she rode too close to the edge. God, this push and pull of his heart when it came to her made his chest ache.

She'd pull him in with her charm, her humor, her easy way of looking at life, and each time he'd swear maybe she'd be the one who could convince him to love another person enough to start—and build—a life with them. After all, they had the foundation of a solid relationship.

Then she'd push him right back out again when she did something stupid like take jobs where people were trying to kill her—and one of these days would succeed. How could he ever love someone like that? Loss was the only outcome.

You're too damn reckless, he'd told her once, about a decade prior.

To you, maybe, but that's not saying much when you won't even jay walk across the side street of your apartment.

No one had ever accused him of being a risk-taker, that was for sure, but when *everyone* in his life had turned out to be one, who was supposed to hold level ground, keep everyone healthy and safe?

It's what his dad *should* have done; he didn't begrudge the man too much—it was his only fault, and a fatal one at that. He also couldn't blame Millie for how he grew up. However, he didn't have to court that side of her, either.

Easier said than done...

His heart pushed against his chest as it had every time he'd thought of her the past week since their kiss. He'd crossed a line with her and there really wasn't any going back now that he knew what she tasted like, felt like, and what that did to his heart. Forget push and pull—it was a damn rodeo beneath his ribs now.

Made worse by the way she avoided him like *he* was the dangerous one.

Millie sprinted off before the sun rose each morning to get in a run before their days got away from them. Then, after dinner and some light chatter in the barn with everyone but him, she'd head to the bunkhouse before him, softly breathing by the time he got in from his evening group therapy. Since she was hired on both as a therapist and trauma doctor, she was only scheduled for two evening sessions a week.

Dex sighed. The thing was, if he ignored the inherent risk Millie posed to his heart, he *missed* her—missed their banter, how her lip pulled between her teeth when she was truly pleased with something, the feel of her against him while he slept…

That last part was a state secret he'd take with him to the grave. The first morning they'd woken up together, he'd been awake long enough to feel her breathing change, to feel her close the millimeters between them. His body reacted almost immediately; he was hard and turned on like he'd never been before, the memory of the passion in their supposedly fake kiss still hot on his lips.

But she'd shifted away and that had been it. Since then, she tucked herself in the farthest corner of the bed, a compact ball of his longing. He'd be a complete jerk if he tried to touch her when it was obvious she wanted to keep her distance.

His phone buzzed on the small table beside his chair. Shoot. It was his alarm for their first trail ride of the season, something he wasn't exactly thrilled about.

He finished his coffee and closed up the office Hearts and Horses had set up for him; even with a fraction of the comfort of his LA office, it had more than enough to do the job. Which said more than a little about how he wanted to live going forward.

Down at the stables, a small crowd formed around the entrance.

"What's going on here?" Dex asked Ray, who stood toward the back, his hand tucked into his jeans pocket and a half smile on his face.

"Take a look." He nodded toward the first stall, and Dex smiled as well.

Millie.

In a fitted black tank top and snug jeans, her hair tied back in a long braid, she looked the part of a cowgirl. A cowgirl who made his own jeans fit a little snugger around the waist.

Damn. She might have been his best friend and off-limits to anything more, but hell if he didn't want to give a roll in the hay with her a try.

That's not true. You want more than that with her.

He swallowed hard. That was impossible, wasn't it? Because as her friend, he could pretend what she did wasn't his concern; as her boyfriend, that would be impossible. Look at Kelsey. He'd cared for her and Emma, had tried to go against his biology and give being a dad a whirl, but in the end, he'd hurt them both with his pervasive fear of something going wrong.

He couldn't do that to Millie, the most important person in his life.

"What's she doing?"

"Taming the untamable," Ray said, tossing Dex a wink. Dex shifted on his feet uncomfortably.

Yeah, she's been doing that a lot lately.

"A new horse?" Dex asked.

"Nah. We've had the mare a while now, but no one can get through to her. Millie's been down here half an hour and already has Elsa breathing normal. She even took a slice of apple from Millie's hand."

Dex relaxed, too, until Elsa flinched and her nostrils flared. His senses went on full alert. Millie didn't know horses any more than he did, but of course, if there was danger or risk, she was front and center.

Millie remained calm and eventually Elsa matched her energy, stilling.

"Wow. I had no idea Millie was so good with horses," Dex said. Awe filled the empty space in his chest, and it overflowed when Millie nodded to Reese Laramy, one of their patients. But the nerves didn't settle. Millie was still in the lion's den.

"Come on in here, Reese," Millie said.

"You've got an amazing woman there, Doc. There's a line out the door for her one-on-ones and she beat Gale at pickleball, so I'm eternally grateful to her for that. He's been insufferable with no one to challenge him here."

Dex considered that. He'd seen Millie army-tough, laying down the law when she needed to. He'd seen her slaphappy and giving him grief for one of his idiosyncrasies. But he'd never seen her so patient, so calm.

He found himself leaning in like the rest of the patients and staff.

"It's okay, she's just got to smell you and get to know your scent from the rest of these guys'," Millie told Reese.

"She won't hurt me?"

"She doesn't want to. She wants to get to know you. But she can see you're gentle, like her. Just a little wild along the edges."

Reese smiled and so did Dex.

"Put your hand out slowly, and leave it palm up so she can take the carrot from you," Millie instructed, demonstrating with her own carrot. "That's it. You're a natural."

Reese smiled under the compliment. She looked… *happy*. All because of Millie.

When Reese got Elsa eating out of her hand, the crowd erupted into hushed cheers and laughter. Reese bowed, which earned a more raucous round of applause.

"Okay, show's over, folks. Time to hit the trails before the only light we have is from the moon."

Everyone nodded and followed Ray into the stables. Dex slid next to Millie, nervous all of a sudden. He'd never been uncomfortable around her, not like this. Part of their friendship was their easy way of falling into step with one another. But faking a marriage while harboring real feelings was getting more and more difficult.

"You were amazing back there."

"Thanks," she said. She didn't glance over at him as she placed the tack on her mare, Tillamook. But the familiar hint of pink traveled up her neck.

"Mind showing me what you're doing so I don't look like an idiot out there?"

"I thought Gale was gonna teach you how to saddle up yesterday."

"He was. But I've worked the past three nights, which you know since you're asleep already when I get home."

"That sounded a little judgmental." She stopped working on the buckle in her hand and gazed at him. Gone was the fire, the spark that had always flitted between them. Replacing it was a nonchalance that hit him like a punch. "Which, frankly, I don't need from you."

What had he done?

"It wasn't. I just miss you, that's all." He rubbed her arm with the back of his hand but she pulled back immediately.

"What's there to miss, Dex?" she asked, turning her attention back to the horse. "This isn't real, so there's no use pretending otherwise when no one's looking. We can just be friends. People who call each other by their last names and steal food off each other's plates. Isn't that enough?"

Dex glanced over her shoulder and sure enough, everyone was busy with their own horses and gear.

"There's more than just a fake relationship here and you know it."

"Yep. We're friends and have been for fifteen years. Don't worry. That hasn't changed."

"Millie—"

"I've got to run. I'm supposed to be working with the patients on being present in every part of this ride, from the gearing up through brushing a horse down after a ride."

"Can we talk later?"

Millie shook her head. "I'm heading out with Ray after dinner for a drink in town since I have tomorrow morning off."

"Seriously? Millie—"

"Have a good ride, Dex."

She led her horse to the other side of the barn, leaving Dex confused for the umpteenth time since they'd arrived in Cambria.

It was time to figure out what was wrong with his wife and just what kind of penance he had to do to fix it. If that meant risking more than he was comfortable with? Well, too bad.

Surely *nothing* could be worse than the feeling in the pit of his stomach, knowing he was disappointing the one person he loved most.

CHAPTER SEVEN

MILLIE ENCOURAGED HER horse into a trot alongside Reese, who continued to wear the smile she'd first shown back at the stables. There'd been a lot Millie wasn't sure about when they took this job—being around patients with similar trauma to her, sharing a bunkhouse and a bed with Dex—but moments like this made it all worth it.

She sighed, thinking back to earlier that morning, to Dex's pained expression when she left on another run and didn't invite him. Yes, even with him, with his constant tempting presence, being here was worth it.

"How're you feeling?" she asked Reese.

"Good. Better. I wasn't sure about this at first. You know, with my leg and all. But it's actually pretty great. My knee doesn't hurt up here."

"That's fantastic. Do me a favor and straighten your bad leg."

Reese shot her a nervous glance, but did as Millie instructed.

"Okay, nice. Your mobility looks good."

From reading Reese's medical chart, Millie knew that was the spot that had absorbed the full impact from the police car chase. Since then, Reese had been reticent to take on new challenges, fearful of the unknown and detached from her physical and mental health.

Right now? Millie didn't see any of that. She knew the benefits of equine therapy for children and folks recovering from alcohol and substance abuse, but to see it working in real time to assist a police officer in overcoming her injuries was pretty incredible.

"Why don't you schedule a consultation with me tomorrow? I'd like to work with you on some exercises that could loosen it up more over time, give you even more range of motion."

"You don't mind? I know you're here to fix our heads and stuff…"

"I don't mind at all. I'm actually double-board certified in trauma medicine and recovery as well as psychiatry."

"Wow. That's cool." Reese whistled, and her horse's ears perked up as she whinnied and shook her head. Reese tensed before Millie could say anything. But it was too late; fear was clear in Reese's eyes, showed in the way her hands gripped the reins.

"It's okay. Buttercup's just nervous. Relax your legs, Reese, and loosen the reins."

Reese shook her head vehemently. "I—I can't."

"You can. You've done much harder things than this, Reese. Remember, Buttercup can feel everything you're feeling, so let's give her a chance to calm down, okay?"

"O-okay."

"Do me a favor and take a deep breath in and then tell me your favorite kind of ice cream."

Millie kept her gaze pinned to Reese's, but didn't miss the way Reese's hands loosened on the reins.

"I don't like ice cream."

"What?" Millie asked, grinning, but pretending to be outraged with her hands on her hips. She was careful to keep her voice even so Buttercup didn't spook again. "You're kidding me."

Reese shook her head, her hands resting on her thighs again like she'd been taught.

"I think we may have to talk about that."

Reese smiled, her shoulders and legs relaxed. Buttercup was back to normal, ambling down the trail like nothing was amiss. Millie breathed in deeply, following her own advice after the near miss. They were almost back to the stables, at least. She glanced ahead and saw an empty stall where Dex's horse, Prince Reginald, was supposed to be.

So he'd made it out, huh?

Curiosity gripped her and after making sure Reese was safely off her horse and promised to see Millie the next day about her leg, Millie took off back down the trail they'd come from. A couple hundred yards in, she caught a glimpse of the dark eyes that haunted her dreams each night she lay less than ten inches from Dex.

Dex chatted with Charlie, a veteran from the coast guard who'd lost 80 percent of his sight during a training exercise gone wrong. He couldn't fly anymore for obvious reasons, but each time Millie had seen him on a horse, he looked content, at least.

"That's interesting," Dex said. He met Millie's gaze and shook his head. He needed to be alone with this patient. She nodded and turned Tillamook back to the stables, listening as she rode. "Tell me more," Dex urged Charlie.

Millie smiled. It was such a simple therapy move, to ask the patient to tell them more, but god was it effective.

Eventually they all made it back to the stables and as everyone else followed Ray to the barn to set up for dinner, Millie and Dex were left alone to hang tack and shut everything off until their next long ride. With only eight weeks until the families came out to visit, they needed all the riding time they could get.

There was one family visit per session where the patients could invite their loved ones to participate in their therapy sessions, meals, even rides through the rolling hills. From what Millie understood, this one would be special since it included a beach ride at White Rock State Marine Conversation Area.

The patients would love the combination of salty sea air—therapeutic in its own right—and the connection to the animals they loved. As long as their regular rides were like today's.

"How's Charlie doing?" Millie asked. She cleaned off a dusty saddle and placed it on the shelf next to the others.

"He's good. Thinks he might try to teach at Embry-Riddle so he's still around pilots and all that."

"That's a great idea. You come up with it?"

"Don't sound so surprised," he said, frowning.

"I'm not." She let out a puff of air. That was the way of things lately—she was constantly holding back when it came to Dex. "I'm sorry, I just… I've been having a rough week," she finally admitted.

His brows furrowed. "Yeah, I know."

"Sorry if that's a problem for you, Dex, but I could do without your anger right now. I know we picked this place for me, that I called in my audible, but I need some time to acclimate."

To living with you as my fake husband while I care about you for real.

"I'm not mad at you for taking some time, Millie." There it was again—the use of her first name, an ounce of tenderness attached. The oscillation gave her whiplash.

"Then why *are* you?" she hissed, lowering her voice when a stable hand walked by. "Because I can read you like a book and you're pissed. At me."

"I am. But only because you're my best friend. And you're treating me like a stranger. You won't talk to me, look at me and you're sure as hell not sharing anything with me anymore. So why am I risking *everything* being here for you when you're treating me like a communicable disease? You don't get to be distant from me after calling in *the* favor, okay?"

She sighed. "I'm sorry." He looked down at her, shock on his open lips. "It's only because I care about you," she said. She couldn't meet his gaze, though. Not without risking everything—specifically, her heart.

"I care about you, too. That's why this whole silent treatment is making me nuts."

"Not—not in *that* way," she whispered. Her voice was almost swallowed up by the evening air that no longer seemed laced with possibility. Now it felt heavy, repressive.

"What do you mean?" he asked. He'd put down the piece of brass he was polishing and walked over to her. Averting her gaze was impossible with him this close, and she felt the heat of his undivided attention. "Millie, talk to me."

He tilted her chin up, and it quivered at his touch. Her eyes watered and his gaze softened.

"Please tell me what you mean by that. Not in *what* way? As friends?"

Millie nodded and then twisted her chin out of his grasp. He caught her cheek with a gentle palm and slowly guided it back to center.

Dex opened and shut his mouth as if he wanted to say something, then he finally shook his head.

Of course he wouldn't feel the same. How could he? He'd said a hundred times over that her life wasn't anything he envied or wanted to be a part of. And he was right—their wants might have been similar, but their needs were polar opposite to one another.

Tears stung the corners of her eyes, blurring her vision. That was the only reason she didn't see Dex inching closer to her until his lips touched hers and heat spread from there across her cheeks, her neck, her chest.

She pulled back, surprise etched in her gaze, her lips tingling where they already missed the feel of his.

"Dex, please don't do this if you're not—"

"Shh…" he said, brushing her lips softly with his again. "Just shut up and kiss me, wife."

Dex spent the next few minutes in absolute bliss. Kissing Millie before had been a chore, something he'd done to protect them—and it had still been the hottest thing he'd ever experienced. But now? When it was his choice? *Her* choice? Damn if he didn't erupt into flames right there in the stables.

His hands finally knew the exquisite pleasure of tangling in her messy curls. His lips and tongue found ways to explore her mouth that hadn't ever occurred to him before. And now he wondered how he'd gone fifteen years—*fifteen years!*—without kissing Millie Tyler every damn day.

She moaned into his mouth, pressing closer to his chest so that only molecules of air separated them. He straddled her legs and cradled her against him.

"Dex," she whispered into the space their mouths shared.

"Millie," he replied.

The dinner bell rang then, loud and unwelcome. The spell was broken and Millie pulled back, breathless and her skin showing all the places the heat flashed against it. God, how he wanted to touch each bloom of heat, kiss each burst of warmth, cherish all of her. Had he been hungry for anything other than more of Millie's kisses before this? He didn't think there'd ever been a time he'd have chosen food over her mouth, her hands.

He released her shoulders and stepped back. Only then did his conscience step in and interrupt his thoughts about how to get his fake wife naked sooner rather than later.

What are you doing? it asked. *She's your best friend and the only person in the world who knows everything about you.*

Wasn't that a reason to keep doing what they were doing?

Why? So you can disappoint her, too? What do you think is going to happen if she wants more than a quickie in the bunkhouse? What if she loves you, huh? Wants you to give more than you're able to? Have you thought about that?

Shit. He hadn't considered what would happen *after* kissing her, but now that was the only thing on his mind. Would his moral compass allow him to pursue her, knowing the risk it posed to their tenuous new start? More importantly, would their friendship survive?

His heart lurched as she smiled up at him. God, he wanted this, even if it was short-lived. They could say it was to keep up appearances, couldn't they? And enjoy the fruits of the lie that had gotten them into this in the first place?

He and Millie were doing more good at the ranch than the construct they'd built would hurt. But if they rode the line between truth and fantasy, what would it do to *Millie*? She'd been burned before; could she separate the lie from reality so soon after losing the only other family she'd ever known when she separated from the army?

She traced her bottom lip with the tip of her finger. He wanted to suck both into his mouth until she cried out with pleasure.

"That was…" she started.

Incredible. Mind-blowing.

"Yeah, it was," he said instead. "We should go."

"Oh, okay." She frowned and he cursed under his breath. *Christ.* With a medical degree from Stanford, he couldn't come up with anything more articulate than that?

"I just mean—"

"Mmm-hmm. It's fine."

"Can we please spend time together after dinner?" he asked.

"You have group therapy and I'm going out."

He sighed. If they really were husband and wife, this schedule would be the quickest route to divorce. "I miss you, Millie."

"You can't miss what you never had." Her voice was so quiet, so filled with anguish, so…not Millie. Was the kiss too much? Was he delusional in thinking she'd kissed him back with the same passion he'd given her?

She strode out of the stables toward the bunkhouse, jogging once she was out of view. Dex watched her until she got to the door, his heart yanking at his chest as she ran.

He started for the barn, tucking his desire away until they got a chance to talk. The facts were simple: they were best friends, she was his only family and he was half of all she had left. Losing her would do him in. Even when she wasn't around, she lit up his thoughts, knowing her sass and sarcasm and brilliance was out there making the world a better place.

Was sex even a pale comparison to all that?

"Hey there, Doc. Mind if I run something by you?" Gale asked the moment Dex walked into the dining space. His gaze scoured the room, looking for the familiar wild curls. He flexed his hands, recalling what those curls had felt like laced between his fingers just moments ago.

"Sure," he said.

Where is she?

"What can I do you for, boss?"

"It's actually a private matter. Can we talk outside real quick?"

"Of course." Dex glanced over his shoulder, but still didn't see Millie. He followed Gale onto the porch, where the waning sun had cooled the coastal ranch temperatures enough that he wished he'd brought a sweater this evening. "Go ahead," he urged Gale.

"It's about Ray."

"Is he okay?" Dex asked. He'd come to respect and like the guy in the short weeks he'd been at Hearts and Horses.

"He's fine, but he's getting antsy. You know, about…" Gale gestured to his left ring finger that was, of course, empty.

"Ray wants a commitment?" Dex asked.

"He does. And he deserves it, but I'm not sure I'm ready."

"For him or for what loving him fully would mean?"

"Hmm. That's a good question. I can't imagine life without the pain in the ass always nagging me to do things better. He's the reason I wake up smiling."

"But?" Dex asked. His thoughts conjured Millie, but he shoved the wispy image of her away until he could focus on it, bring it to life. It didn't sate the ache in his chest, though.

Gale shook his head. "When I say that out loud, the *but* doesn't seem as powerful."

"That's a good sign, but it's still there, I'm guessing, and not talking about it will only give it power."

"Fair enough. Okay, well, here it is." Gale shoved his hands in his pockets and glanced around him as if to make sure they were alone. When Dex followed his gaze, he caught sight of Millie leaving the bunkhouse, and even in the dim light, he could see the puffiness under her eyes, the damp red on her cheeks. She'd been crying.

Dex shook his head. He couldn't be in two places at once. He'd connect with her after Gale was done.

"I love Ray, I do. But once we sign, seal and make this rodeo official, well…" He trailed off, his pained gaze set on the dining hall. Dex could relate.

"You're responsible for someone else's happiness?"

"Exactly. And I've been running this place for too long to know that's not how it goes, not really, anyway. No one can make you happy but yourself, but I've got a long way to go with my own mental and physical rehab. What if we take this on too soon and I wrap him in my mess?"

Dex widened his stance, looked at Gale through appraising eyes. "Have you yet?"

"No, or at least, I don't think so. If anything, he's calmed me down, made me better."

Again, Dex found himself nodding, not because Gale's admission was revelatory with what he'd assumed of his and Ray's relationship, but because it shined a light on how Dex felt for Millie. It was as if Gale held up a mirror for Dex to gaze into the whole time he spoke.

"Then, you have your answer, don't you?"

However, the question remained: would Dex take his own advice?

"Thanks, Doc. This is what I needed."

"No sweat. Hey, speaking of, I might beg you for an evening off one day next week so Millie and I can connect about our days before she's too exhausted to do much but snore me into submission," Dex said, only half joking about the second part. Millie was gorgeous, brilliant, funny and the kindest person he knew...but she could put grown men to shame with the way she sawed logs.

"Consider it done. Both things. I'll make sure you share a few evenings off, and now that you've met with all the patients we have here, we'd like to have you on a more consistent five-day workweek."

"Thanks, Gale. That'll be nice." The men walked into the barn, where the delectable scent of fried chicken and corn bread filled the space. So did the sounds of laughter and pleasant conversation. Dex inhaled it all as he watched his and Millie's patients all chatting and talking about their days.

This. This was what Dex had been missing at Mercy Hospital. The connection, the camaraderie, the community of healing. Maybe he'd have stayed if they would have followed through on funding a program like this there. One that would help trauma victims from the area in a safe, all-inclusive space that paid attention to the whole patient, not just their injuries.

Even Millie was animatedly discussing something with Reese. The remnants of whatever had upset her were almost invisible, but Dex knew what to look for and found it in the way her smile didn't meet her eyes, in the way she picked at the corner of her lip.

Still, she was stronger than she'd been three months ago.

No matter what happened between them, this was a good move, for that reason alone. But that didn't mean he should give in to his desire. He cared for Millie a whole hell of a lot, but Gale's words rang loud in his ears. What if he let her in and took her down with the parts of himself that were barely healed?

He sighed. Longing washed through him, but it wasn't worth the risk. Millie was off-limits not only because of their different lifestyles but because he couldn't imagine what it would be like to have everything in his arms and lose it because he turned out to be too damn broken to really love anyone.

Millie wouldn't be collateral damage in his war against demons that weren't quite out of his rearview.

CHAPTER EIGHT

DEX'S EVENING THERAPY sessions had gone pretty well, considering he was mildly distracted by thoughts of Millie. All throughout dinner, she'd ignored him, laughing with Reese and Ray as if nothing were wrong.

As if he hadn't caught her drying her eyes coming out of the bunkhouse.

"Dr. Shaw, you're an incredible asset to these guys," Ray said, walking up beside Dex. For a man with a severe injury, he didn't let it slow him down. He kept pace with everyone on the ranch and had even had a horse saddle made to accommodate his prosthetics.

"Thanks, Ray. They're pretty great. Making good progress, too. Which I actually wanted to talk to you about."

"Shoot."

Dex glanced up at the moon. It was still only a sliver, but without lights from a city, it cast a pale glow over the camp, bathing it in blue. He had to admit, though the city had always held his dreams and aspirations, the resources he'd thought he needed, this life gave him a peace of mind he hadn't found elsewhere. Maybe Millie was on to something.

"Everett and Tom aren't where I want them to be."

"Mmm. How so?"

"Well, neither has accepted where they've been or what they need to do in order to form healthy relationships in the future. Having their families here in a couple weeks without much change is gonna be tough. Maybe a setback."

"I agree. Let's talk about that at our staff meeting Monday."

Dex nodded his agreement. "I'd actually like to get them working the stables and managing the schedule down there. They've both got the experience, and are excited about the animals, which means they'll be motivated to do right by them."

"I'll run it up the Gale pole, but I think that sounds like a great idea. Thanks for thinking of it. See what I mean? You and Millie are good for these folks."

"I appreciate it." Dex spared a glance toward the bunkhouse. He was glad for the way the thin moon and starless night sucked the color from the landscape because he was sure his cheeks were flashing red. If only he could be good for Millie.

"Everything okay on the home front?" Ray asked.

Dex fidgeted with a coin in his pocket.

"Yeah, we're just figuring out how to work together and keep the romance alive, too," Dex lied. What was one more in the pile they'd amassed? "But Gale's scheduled a shared day off for the latter."

Ray considered him a moment, his gaze steely, even in the waning light.

"I get that," he finally said. "I'll make sure you get time without patients to touch base about work, too. Striking this balance will be key to all of us staying sane and keeping our significant others happy."

"I appreciate it. I'm sure Millie will, too."

Would she, though? More time with him might set her off like their kiss had earlier that day. Maybe if he could keep his libido in check...

Dex waved and headed back to the bunkhouse, his heart heavy. Heavy and split in two. On one hand, he was happier than he'd been in a while, more fulfilled professionally, too. Here were patients who *needed* them and the work he and Millie were doing.

On the other hand, he was wading in dangerous territory, going against what he knew was good for him. His growing—and surprising—feelings for Millie were going to burn them both. He wasn't equipped to show and give love, especially to someone whose life of danger and risk drudged up all too familiar fears stemming from his tumultuous childhood.

Faking it for the sake of their jobs was only adding to the pile of guilt.

He leaned his forehead against the door, his shoulders sagging with indecision.

"I wish I could love you the way you deserve," he whispered against the sturdy oak door.

He opened it, careful with his footsteps so he didn't wake Millie, whose back was to him. Her smooth bare skin exposed by the tank top she wore to bed appeared to glow under the moonlight streaming in through the windows.

His fists clenched, a feeble attempt to quelch his desire to run his fingers along the curve of her.

Good grief, what was he thinking, agreeing to be her fake husband? The unmet desire alone would run him ragged over the next few months. Because somewhere in the stolen glances and touches, the longing had become very freaking real.

"Oh, Millie," he whispered soft enough for the early night breeze to take the words away, "I love you, but I'm not sure it's enough."

She stirred, but didn't roll over. He slipped out of his shoes and clothes, then brushed his teeth and got into bed beside Millie.

Her eyes fluttered open, then. "How was the therapy session?" she asked.

"Good." He resisted the urge to lean over and kiss her, the pull on him so real and so damn tempting. "I'll fill you in when we wake up, or maybe when we have the time off together to consult on patient progress."

He gave in to his desire, halfway at least, tucking one of Millie's curls behind her ear.

"Mmm… That'll be nice. I'm exhausted."

"I know. Go back to sleep, hun."

His lips twisted into a scowl. He hadn't meant to let that last word slip.

She caught the error and her eyes grew wide, her lips softened into an *O*.

"Sorry," he whispered.

"Don't be," she replied, her voice as faint as the

ambient light from outside. "I like the sound of the word on your lips."

Millie shifted under the covers and her leg rested against Dex's.

Damn. He was hard as the ground outside just seeing her pale skin bathed in moonlight. The caress of her smooth skin under the covers was enough to eradicate any self-control he had left.

"What are you doing?" he asked. His heart pounded in the silence.

"Do you not want me to?"

Her foot ran up his calf, finally hooking around his thigh and Dex emitted a low growl.

"What I want and what we need aren't the same thing, Mil."

Even in the fractured dark, he could see her draw her bottom lip between her teeth. Her palm rested on his bicep and then trailed along his shoulder. Her words from the stables echoed in the liminal space between them.

I care about you. More than a friend.

"Haven't you wondered what this might be like?"

Dex gulped nothing but dry air, the moisture drained from his throat. He had. Often. But it always ended in the same conclusion—they'd probably have run their course by now, her bored of his control freak tendencies, and he'd be without her amazingness. Amazingness he was attracted to. What a damn double-edged sword.

"I have, but that doesn't mean we should act on it."

"Why not?"

A thousand reasons.

Not the least of which was the fact that she wanted more from him than he could give.

"You're my best friend," he settled on. But the way her fingers brushed his jawline, then tangled in his hair said she was capable of more than that.

Good God, he wanted to know more—what she tasted like, felt like pressed against him…

How could he act on his basest desires with a woman he cherished for so many other reasons? He loved her, sure, but loving Millie in the way she deserved meant taking on risk he couldn't stomach.

On the other hand, how was he supposed to resist making love to her, especially when she was offering herself up to him on a silvery blue-tinted platter?

"What we need might be to get this out of our systems," she whispered. "Maybe if we give in to whatever this is building between us, we can go back to being just friends."

A one-night stand? With his best friend? The idea had merit.

Millie pulled him closer so their hips were aligned. No way now she couldn't tell how badly he did, indeed, want this since his erection pressed against her.

"You make a good point."

She rocked into him.

"So do you, it seems," she said, her smile mischievous but her eyes focused with desire.

It was all he needed to give in. The consequences

couldn't be greater than living in purgatory with her the next five months.

"Come here, wife," he said, pulling her the rest of the way on top of him. "I think it's high time we consummate this marriage."

She giggled until he kissed her, and then it was as if a match had been lit in a room filled with fumes of longing. They exploded, their kisses and hands hungry for more. When he teased her mouth open, she moaned into him, flicking his lips with her tongue.

She tasted like mint but the scent of plumeria from her shampoo was what almost undid him. He breathed her in and committed that scent to memory, as if he'd ever be able to forget a moment of this.

Dex's hands wrapped along the curve of her jaw, his fingers clasping around the base of her head as he let his tongue explore her mouth. Her own hands traced down his chest, then stopped as she reached the part of him so filled with wanting it was about to burst. She took him in her hands, firm and strong, moving over him until he groaned.

"Please," he begged. "I want you so damn bad, Millie."

"Show me how much," she whispered against his ear before tracing it with her tongue.

He flipped her on her back, eliciting a squeal of delight. "Careful what you wish for, Millie Tyler." Starting at her neck, he kissed along her collarbone, sucking the curve of her shoulder while she rocked underneath him.

"Yes," she uttered.

Taking that as a sign of encouragement, he peppered her chest with kisses, too, stopping to pull each of her nipples into his mouth so he could tease them with his tongue. She cried out, but he wasn't close to done. He wanted to taste each curve, each swathe of her bare skin. He wanted to make her feel what he felt every time he looked at her.

Had he wondered what loving her would be like? Only every minute of the past few months.

He traced her belly button with his finger as his mouth closed over one of her breasts. She screamed out his name and he couldn't hold back a grin.

"Shh…" he teased her. "You'll wake the neighbors." He took the other breast into his mouth, giving it the same attention.

"Eff the neighbors. I want you inside me," she moaned.

Goddamn, had he ever wanted anything so badly? But not yet. Not until he'd left her satisfied and sated.

His tongue moved down her body, drawing shapes on her hips. When he moved to the small swathe of hair covering her sex, her breath halted. Dex waited for the exhale as he ran his tongue up her center, and when it came, so did she. Her body shook with the aftereffects, but she opened her eyes and met his gaze.

"Take me," she whispered, her lips quivering.

He reached into the stand beside his bed and procured a condom, sheathing himself and then thrusting into her in one movement. She screamed, her hands gripping the pillow behind her head.

"Goddamn, Dex," she cried out. His name on her lips while he rocked in and out of her warmth almost made him come right there. "I want you to come."

He dipped down and kissed her, softer and deeper this time.

"I'm close." His breath was tight, his whole body on edge as he moved against the beautiful woman beneath him.

"Come for me, Dex," she urged. When he did, she tightened around him, her own body shaking against his. He held tight to her, kissing her gently between shuddering breaths. She curled against him and he rolled to his back so he could tuck her in the nook of his shoulder and chest.

His lips lightly grazed the top of her head and he brushed the damp curls from her face.

She relaxed against him, her arm draped over his chest, her legs tangled in his, and they lay that way for minutes. Not talking, just…being. He sighed. The eventual soft purr of her breathing said she'd fallen asleep, but it wouldn't be that easy for him.

He squeezed her tighter to his body, desperate to shake the feeling that had come over him after making love to his best friend.

She'd claimed it would be just the thing to get rid of whatever sexual tension was building between them, and she'd been right—the tension was gone. But what replaced it was far worse. Because it hadn't done a damn thing to quench his desire for her.

No, if anything, it made him want more of her—*all* of her—and the problem with that was simple. There was no way their friendship was going to remain unscathed.

Millie lay awake, staring at the wall. Or, the part of the wall she could see over the arc of Dex's sculpted chest. God, she should be exhausted, given her day and the night that followed, but a frenetic energy buzzed through her veins. She'd been awake when Dex came in and his whispers still haunted her.

He loved her. Just not enough. *Enough for what,* she wanted to ask.

In the end, it hadn't mattered. She'd made her case—internally arguing that sating a physical desire had worked in the past to keep unwanted feelings at bay—and they'd given in to each other. Millie finally knew the divine pleasure of his lips, his hands, his... Well, *all* of him.

But damn. Her tried and true one-night stand approach hadn't worked. Not one little bit.

Her fingers traced the definition in his muscles, awe at the perfection of them hitting her on multiple levels. Speaking as a physician, he was an Adonis sculpture like those she'd studied in medical school. Perfect, symmetrical, ideal in all the right ways.

But as a woman, all she saw and felt beneath her was a work of art.

I just made love to Dexter Shaw.

Her best friend, her only family, her fake husband. Those lines were blurred to hell now.

Heat crept along her skin as she recalled what loving him had been like. His hands caressing every inch of her, his mouth on places she'd only dreamed he'd kiss one day, the rest of him filling her like he was the missing piece to her anatomy.

I just made love to Dexter Shaw, she repeated.

Unfortunately, it came with an addendum this time.

For the first and only time.

After all, that was the agreement they'd made. Once, to get it out of their systems. Who knew it would be like that cheesy potato chip advertisement from the '80s and once wouldn't be near enough to satisfy her.

Because—*whoa!* The man was the best sex of her *life*. She swallowed a scream of injustice that she'd discovered this about her best friend, the only man she knew who was off-limits.

Dex shifted beneath her, stretching. He groaned and then turned his gaze to hers, which she was wholly unprepared for. She'd expected sweet, maybe reticent, but the heat wafting off him was palpable and she was suddenly grateful for the windows they kept open at night.

"Good morning, gorgeous," he said, his voice still thick with sleep. He pulled her tighter to him and kissed the top of her head before tilting her chin up so he could do the same to her lips. Her greedy lips that craved more.

What is he doing? It was only supposed to be the once.

Shut up, she told her brain. As Dex's hands slid around her waist, cupping her butt and drawing her on top of him, it wasn't the time to listen to that particular organ.

Millie deepened the kiss, drawing Dex's tongue out to tangle with hers. When he reached for the nightstand drawer again, she whispered, "I'm covered that way."

"And I'm clean."

"Then leave it. I want to feel you."

Dex wasted no time releasing her onto him, filling her again. She moaned with pleasure, lifting herself just enough so the tip of him remained buried in her, then she sank back, taking him back in. He peppered her chest, her shoulder, the nape of her neck with kisses until she felt wholly, fully cherished.

"You're perfect," he whispered against her hair.

I want this forever, she wanted to say.

"I'm close," she answered instead.

"Come, babe. I want you to come."

He thrust harder, faster, until she squeezed around him, coming to orgasm. She gasped, digging her nails into his back. He rocked his hips deeper, moaning with pleasure as he joined her.

Afterward, they lay on top of one another, sweaty despite the almost frigid air blowing in. Millie's head rested on his chest while he ran his fingers through her tangled curls.

"We sorta broke our rule," she whispered.

"I don't count this. We're in the same bed we went to sleep in, so it's technically not a second time."

She giggled, but sobered when his hand tightened around her. Her eyes squeezed shut. All she wanted was this, forever. But that was impossible. Her best friend could be her lover, but that was it. He didn't want more, or at least he hadn't three or four orgasms ago. It wasn't like she didn't know why—he'd lost every important person in his life and the fear shaped every choice he made.

She had her own demons, too. When her mom had passed at the same age as Dex had been when he lost his father, she'd thought her father's marriage to a new woman would fix the hurt; instead it made her life a living hell—a hell she'd been in until she met Dex on her first pre-deployment leave. So, how could she risk their friendship for sex?

It's more than that, all her organs agreed.

Ugh. All she knew with certainty was that she didn't want this to end.

"We should get up and get ready. You've got a full day and I'm using my morning off to run some errands if you need anything in town."

Millie tried to slide off Dex's torso, but he kept her pinned in place.

"What if," he said, shifting so they could see each other. His bottom lip was tucked between his teeth. Was Dexter Shaw *nervous*? "What if we made a pact?"

Millie sat up and draped her arms over her bare

breasts. Somehow, in the light of day, the pillow talk seemed more intimate than what they'd done the night before. And that morning.

"What kind of pact?"

Dex sat up as well, leaning against the headboard, his arms languidly crossed behind his head. He looked like a damn model for underwear or something. Only the way he bit the corner of his lip and the subtle way he couldn't hold her gaze said he was anything other than at peace.

"Well, I was thinking about it. What kind of married couple are we, not kissing and holding hands and stuff in public?"

"We're not in public. We're at work."

Her heart screamed something that made her stomach flip over itself a couple times. She ignored it.

"Agreed, but why don't we lean into the thing we're selling? You know, go for it while we're here."

"You mean, be a real couple?"

He stiffened, but then relaxed just as quickly. "Sure, yeah. While we're here, anyway. We know we work as friends and colleagues. We found out last night that it extends to the bedroom, so why sell ourselves short? Let's just enjoy what we have for the next five-plus months and then we can reevaluate when the contract's up. Think of it as *leveling up* our friendship, even if it would be a disaster in the real world."

She didn't mention that this *was* the real world, that the lie didn't change anything but others' perspectives of their relationship.

On the surface, his level-up idea made sense. Hell, she wanted it as much as she'd ever wanted anything. But just below the surface, the tepid truth lay waiting. Now she understood the tremble in his lips. If they did this and messed it up…

"If I don't find something permanent, I'm headed to Doctors Without Borders after this."

He frowned. "I know."

"And you've got no interest in traveling for work. You want your stability."

"I know that, too, Millie. Do you not want to do this, because—"

"No," she shot back. She placed a hand on his chest. "I do. I just want to make sure if we do this, we do it with our eyes open to reality."

"Sure. Of course. I know we're different, Millie, that we have different goals in life. It's why we haven't done this sooner, right?"

The breath was knocked out of her chest with the admission.

"Is that why?" she asked. "It's not because you can't have someone rely on you? Or because you just saw me as a friend?"

Dex drew her in close to him. "Millie, I've always been curious about us. And friend or not, you've always been hot." He grinned, though it didn't assuage the unease in her chest. "But you're right; I worried about my own limitations and what I had to offer you. I still do. This little pact could give us time to explore more, though."

Explore more.

That was the problem. She didn't want more; when it came to Dex, she wanted *everything*.

"And if one of us wants more after this?" Not just from one another, but from life? Because one thing was still unequivocally true about her best friend—he'd never want any risks in his professional life, either.

"Then we talk about it like adults. Listen to one another like we have since we met."

"You didn't exactly listen to everything. I gave you a treatment plan to follow and you all but told me to go to hell."

"I didn't know what a brilliant doctor you were back then." He smiled and kissed her lightly on the lips.

God. This was all she wanted—the ease and perfection of loving her best friend and having him love her in return.

"And now?" she asked, gazing up at him.

"Well, we've established your brilliance, obviously. But I don't know that I ever thanked you for that day."

"The day we met? You did. Multiple times. And I called in the favor, so we're good."

"No, Millie, I mean for how you upended my life that day. You know I'm crap when it comes to relationships, but not just the romantic ones. You coming into my life showed me I'm capable of so much more than I give myself credit for. I can care for someone and take the risk that comes with it." Millie pressed her forehead against Dex's chest, letting the warmth of his words and skin take away the chill his "pact" gave her. "And it looks like you're not done doing that, either."

He bent down and kissed her. His hands were tender where they'd been hungry, his mouth passionate where it had been desperate. On paper, this was exactly what Millie craved from him—the desire bleeding into their fifteen years of friendship. They'd earned this, hadn't they?

That doesn't mean it's any more real now than it was last night. Your relationship is still built on a sham.

Millie ignored her pesky, obtrusive subconscious.

Her relationship *status* might be a fraud, but that didn't mean her relationship was. There was a reason she and Dex had decided to do this at all— besides the favor she called in. They shared a genuine friendship that spanned far longer than most folks' actual marriages.

As Dex deepened the kiss and she let his hands explore the places he knew would drive her to distraction, faces flashed behind her eyelids.

Reese. Charlie. Dominic. *Ray and Gale.*

If she was wrong and this backfired, what she risked was *so much* greater than just her heart. Somehow, unexpectedly, she'd stumbled into another family, and losing this one would do real damage.

CHAPTER NINE

DEX WENT THROUGH the next five weeks of work in a daze. A sex-induced daze, but still. Twelve-hour shifts—including the promised time to share notes with Millie on their patients' progress—were bookended by lovemaking sessions with his fake-wife-but-real-girlfriend. It was like trying to sate an unquenchable thirst.

Dex simply couldn't get enough of her.

And yeah, he was well aware of how problematic that was. Because it wasn't just sex—*damn good sex*—to him. *Feelings* were involved. Big messy ones that looked a lot like the ones on the end of Cupid's arrow and started with a capital *L*.

Shit.

On one hand, that was a good thing. He cared enough about another person—a person whose needs and safety he wanted to put in front of his own—to feel something other than abject horror at the idea of spending a life with them.

Dex Shaw was capable of a relationship.

On the other hand, boy, had he picked wrong. Millie Tyler was all sorts of bad for him when it came to making him feel safe. Twice that week she'd gone on a solo run and come back with stories of a cool snake she saw. Three times, she'd burned herself at the campfire, and once on the hot plate where she made them tea at night. Then there were the constant conversations at work; he'd caught snippets of what she'd encountered overseas and it wasn't pretty. Bombs, tribal wars and insurgents were the norm.

The black tendrils of his anxiety hadn't come back, but he knew they were close by.

How was he supposed to *ever* sit back and watch this woman he lov—*cared for* get hurt? And to make matters worse, he'd found a pamphlet for DWB in her dresser drawer that morning when he'd gone looking for the underwear she sent him to find. It was next to the front page of their contract, with the end date in bold.

Three months, three weeks and six days left.

It was a countdown for him, too. But he wasn't sure to what anymore.

"Shoot," she muttered, looking down at her finger before sucking on the tip of it.

"What'd you do?" he asked. His pulse raced.

"Just snagged it on this clip. I'm fine."

He exhaled. *He* wasn't fine. Sexually satisfied? *Yes. Absolutely.* Happy? *Mostly.* But calm and fine? *Nope.*

"I'm glad Tom and Everett get some time with their families this weekend," she said, closing the door on his worry about her for the time being. It never stayed shut long, though. She consistently pushed against one of his self-made barriers—this time it was his peace of mind. One of these days, she wouldn't be fine—she'd be really hurt, and he'd be irrevocably devastated.

He sighed, earning him a kiss. *That*, he didn't mind. "Yeah. Me, too."

They'd changed the therapy and treatment protocols for Tom and Everett and both men were looking forward to a truncated weekend with family in a few days. They weren't ready to share beyond an afternoon, but even that was headway.

They just had to get through the moonlit ride along the beach first.

Millie's excitement about the trip was palpable. According to her, this was the most romantic idea anyone had ever had. Not to Dex. Taking a half-ton animal along a dark poorly lit beach with unpredictable tides and keeping track of twenty trauma patients with various mental health triggers wasn't Dex's idea of romance.

It was the kind of thing that kept a trauma doc like her in business.

"I love the ocean at night. There's something therapeutic about the dark skies and the sound of the water crashing against the shore."

He gave a half-hearted laugh. He might not agree, but he'd buy stock in anything that made Millie smile like she was.

"See, when you say the word *crashing*, it loses some of its appeal. And here I thought *therapy* was therapeutic."

She nudged him playfully with her shoulder while they gathered tack in the waning daylight. The staff would join them after dinner to prep the horses, but until then, it was nice to be alone with Millie. That didn't happen often during work hours.

"Ha ha, mister. You know what I mean. To be alone with your thoughts and nature—it's calming." She ran a hand along the leather saddle she carried. He leaned over the pile of brass and kissed her.

"Yeah, if nature behaves. She's a fickle beast, though."

"Maybe, but she's still beautiful. You know, I'd love to sleep under the stars with you one night. It's romantic—I don't care what you say."

He tried for a smile, even a half-hearted one, but shuddered as he recalled the nights he'd slept under the overpass the first month after he ran away from the system, and later for almost a year when he'd been an eighteen-year-old without a plan.

It was the only story Millie didn't know about him, the only one he'd never shared with anyone. No one quite understood how quickly it could all be taken away. Not even Millie, or she'd also understand why he worried every time she got so much as a papercut.

LA was supposed to have mild winters, but that first year of homelessness he'd almost lost a toe and some fingers to frostbite thanks to an unexpected—and unwelcome—cold front. The ER doc on call who had helped bring his limbs back to life had offered him a glimpse at another world, one where nice things and creature comforts were an everyday occurrence. The doc had been caring and kind, answering all Dex's questions about what his job entailed, even laying out a ten-year plan on the back of a blank chart, which Dex still had back in LA, in case Dex wanted to pursue medicine.

In case? Dex was baited, hooked and reeled in.

With four words—*you've got promise, kid*—the doc had covered Dex's bill under a pro bono case, then left in a Porsche with one of the nurses in the passenger seat.

That was all Dex needed to change course. That, and the list of shelters the doctor gave him so he'd have a safe warm place to stay while he put his plan into action.

He'd gotten his GED, applied to a community college and never spent a night outside after that, not even to camp. The rest was history.

If Millie knew the secret shame he kept from her—he had been homeless and a runaway, not some tormented kid with daddy issues like she believed—would she want anything to do with him?

But at the same time, he had a hard time denying her anything.

"We'll see." He kissed her forehead. "For now, let's get ready to lead half a dozen traumatized first responders through the dark on uneven ground with beasts that could spook at the sound of their own tails swishing."

"Look at my boyfriend, the incurable romantic."

Millie dipped lower and kissed Dex on the cheek, then the lips, eliciting a smile from him even as he looked over their shoulders.

"We're alone. Don't worry."

"You want to know what I think is romantic?" he asked.

"What's that?"

He slipped a finger beneath the thin strap of her

tank top and slid it down along the fabric until his hand reached the curve of her breast peeking out from the top of the shirt. She inhaled a sharp breath but didn't answer.

"You," he said, tugging on the strap, pulling her close enough that he could kiss her shoulder. His lips traced the edge of the shirt, until he got to the rise of her breast. Pulling the cotton down, he peppered her exposed flesh with kisses until he reached her nipple. He sucked it into his mouth and teased it with his tongue until she groaned with pleasure.

"Dex," she whispered on an exhale. "We can't. We're in public."

Dex flicked her bud with his teeth and she gasped, arching her back, giving him better access to her. He didn't respond to her worry—or his. Instead, he moved to her other breast and gave it equal attention, the allure of the outdoors Millie had been preaching suddenly making sense.

This *was* kind of therapeutic, being in the semi-covered space, the wind tickling his skin. Taking Millie in his mouth, pleasuring her while the thought of keeping their tryst quiet consumed them both.

It was a risk he was comfortable taking.

When he unbuttoned her jeans and slid his hand along her sex, she gasped.

"We can't," she said, her words broken by each ragged breath she drew in. Yet, when he lifted her shirt, she arched her back to allow him access to her. In times like these, lost in lust, he could almost pretend no outside danger waited in the wings. He could picture being happy with Millie…forever.

"Let me," he whispered, kissing down her stomach while he tugged her jeans and underwear over her hips and knees. She nodded and her approval stoked the fire of desire in him. His thumbs pressed into the hollows of her hips and he lifted her so her back lay against the soft give of the barn blankets they'd just laundered.

Dex trailed his tongue along her hip bone and Millie moaned softly.

"Shhh, darling. I'm going to make you come with my tongue but you can't make a sound, okay?"

She nodded and sucked her bottom lip between her teeth. Dex wasted no time kissing her chill-dimpled skin until he came to her center. He ran a finger along her opening, teasing her wide for him. She tensed, but didn't make a sound.

His tongue ran the length of her before sucking and pulling at her bud. Millie's back arched and her fingers tangled in his hair as he spread her legs wide. His hands caressed her until they came to her full exposed breasts. He cupped them, teasing her tight nipples with his thumb and finger. His tongue darted inside her warm fleshy folds and his thumb strummed at her core until she bucked beneath him. Her breaths became shallow and quick as he sped up his kisses. Suddenly, her hands froze and her body rocked with breathless release.

He didn't stop, just kept kissing her as wave after wave of pleasure rolled through her.

I could get used to this.

When her body calmed and her breaths evened, he pulled her down onto his lap and held her.

"That was nice," she said, her voice as soft as the new barn kittens' fur. He liked all versions of Millie—the ass-kicking side, the part of her that always knew just what to say to make him laugh the moment he took a drink of something. Hell, he even loved the side of her that craved adventure and danger—even though it was diametrically opposed to what made him feel safe. But he had to admit, he *really* liked the sexually satisfied, soft and reticent Millie, too.

"Nice, huh? Looks like I'll have to work a little harder, then," he teased, bending down to her stomach and kissing it until she squealed.

"Please, no. I can barely stand as it is."

That's more like it.

Her skin was flushed and small beads of moisture traced her cheekbones as he helped her stand.

Goddamn, she's gorgeous.

"You know, we have a little time," she said, unbuckling his jeans, her eyes wide and her lips shining with moisture as she gazed up at him. "Let me return the favor."

Dex's breath caught in his chest as her hand cupped his hard length over his pants, caressing it. When it slipped between his skin and boxer briefs, he groaned. The woman knew what she was doing.

"Jesus, Millie."

Her hand wrapped around his girth and stroked him up and down with a firm grip.

His head rolled back and heat flushed his veins.

The distant sounds of the dining hall screen door and voices floating back to the bunkhouse broke the spell almost instantly. The patients would be headed down to the stables shortly. Dex pulled back, forcing Millie to release him.

"Shit," he grumbled, fumbling with his zipper.

"We're fine," she said, reaching for him again.

"No. We should get going. We wouldn't want Ray to ask us why we're behind with the gear. He might not like the answer." Disappointment settled in his chest, even though he tried to keep his voice light. Not at needing to stop Millie from what she'd been doing, but at the idea that twenty patients were about to descend into their quiet private space. He *liked* being alone with her, her humor, her sass... More and more each day.

But the outside world would eat them alive.

He pulled her underwear and pants up and kissed her stomach as he straightened her shirt.

"Yeah, that would be bad," she said, helping him up. "But if anyone understood, it would be Ray. What do you want to bet he and Gale have done the same thing?"

"Oh, I'm not taking a losing bet. I *know* they have."

They laughed.

"Rain check, then?" she asked.

"Abso-freaking-lutely."

Millie wrapped her arms around Dex, squeezing him tight. The sudden seriousness threw him.

"What was that for?" he asked.

She gazed up at him and the thrilling heat from earlier was replaced with a tenderness that almost put him on his ass.

"I just…" She dropped her gaze. "I like this. Whatever this thing is between us. I was worried if we gave us a shot, I'd lose my best friend, but all I did was gain someone to kiss and do dirty stuff with."

The levity at the end of her small speech was so *Millie*. She always found a way to make light of a serious topic. It didn't shroud the heaviness of what she'd been alluding to, though.

"I like it, too," he lied. Because he didn't just *like* it. He'd come to depend on her arms around him at the end of the day. On her kisses to wake him up each morning. On her words to soothe his ragged thoughts.

But one small nagging thought took root and grew in his head as he held her tight to his chest. The greatest risk he'd ever taken was about to blow up in his face, because he had no idea what would happen in just under four months when she walked away from him, toward the one iteration of her future he couldn't follow.

Millie inhaled deeply. The moonlight reflected off the water in shimmery fragments, making it appear that the ocean surface was dappled with small tea lights for miles. It was breathtaking.

Breathtaking in a different way than her experience earlier in the stables, of course. But now that the memory had weaseled its way to the front of her thoughts… Just thinking about it left her feeling warm despite the cool ocean breeze rippling over her skin.

Dex had gone down on her in the middle of the stables, a scene that would keep her giggling when she was old and senile in a nursing home somewhere. But it wasn't that part of the night that lingered on her tongue like the last of a favorite dessert.

It was holding him, feeling the strength of his physicality matched by their shared vulnerability. Maybe it was just her, but she felt like something had shifted tonight, like a lock clicking into place.

But…for what door? And what did it unlock? If it was a lifetime of trust and joy with this man, then she'd gladly open it. Though there were a hundred other possibilities. Like a door that led right to a repeat of her lonely past if things went wrong. Or one that opened to the worry that falling for Dex would tie her down. Fear knocked around in her chest.

"I'd know that smile anywhere," a familiar voice said. Ray rode up beside her and she grinned, happy to see him even if the rest of her life was a confusing mess at the moment.

"Well, hey there, stranger. And what was that about my smile?"

"It's just nice to see the smile of a woman still in love after five years of marriage. That's usually when folks give up and head for the hills."

"Oh, I, uh—" she started, before cutting herself off. She couldn't really refute that, or Ray might read into it. But what he said wasn't true, was it? Was she…*in love*?

She swallowed a groan. That would be so damned inconvenient, especially with so many unanswered questions. Her pulse sped up and she recognized the physical signs of elevated blood pressure.

"Yeah, you know Dex and me," she hedged. "Anyway, I was hoping you'd make it out with us. What was the holdup?"

"Oh, just a quick chat with Tom to get him comfortable with a new horse. No biggie," Ray said, taking the bait she'd laid for switching the topic off her and Dex.

"I hope you don't mind me saying, but Ray, you're glowing."

Ray let out a wistful sigh.

"Yes, I guess you're right." If Millie was seeing things right in the dim blue light, Ray actually blushed. "It's Gale. He's been communicative, observant and even—" he lowered his voice, a conspiracy building "—*romantic*." Ray and Millie both laughed.

She glanced up the beach at Dex, who rode next to George Dominic. The two were laughing under the moonlight and she didn't need the romantic atmosphere to feel a tug at her heart watching him at work. Ray's words came back to her like she'd been shocked with an AED.

Was what she was feeling *love*? How would she even know? It's not like she'd ever experienced anything like it.

Before she could delve too deeply into that particular trauma of hers, Gale rode up beside Millie.

"Mind if I steal my beloved?" he asked.

Ray shot her a look and mouthed, *See?*

She just smiled and shrugged. She was happy the two of them had found their stride.

She and Dex had, too, but that was what worried her. They were fully living in the present, but the future—and their separate goals—would smack them upside the heart sooner than either would realize. Maybe it was time they talked. Like about the half-ton horse-sized topic neither of them wanted to broach.

Wouldn't he have said something already if he wanted more with her—professionally and personally—after this six-month contract? The clock was ticking…

The unknowns with him were scarier than heading into combat, more terrifying than saying goodbye at her father's funeral.

She nudged Tillamook to trot up toward Dex, who was actually heading back to her. "What's up?" she asked. "You okay?"

"Yep, but keep a low profile. I'm on a secret mission." Dex held up his cell phone, which was set to video mode. He was confident and relaxed on his horse, another shift of late.

Millie glanced to where Dex's gaze landed. Gale and Ray were falling behind.

"Wait, is Gale—"

"Yep," Dex said, a wide smile on his face. "He

sure is. And he asked me to film it. Keep an eye on things up here?"

She nodded. "Sure. Of course."

Her stomach flipped and the nerve endings along her skin felt too sensitive all of a sudden. The cool air blowing across her arms made her itchy and uncomfortable.

She glanced back, after checking on the riders, to see Gale—or the hazy silhouette of him swathed in moonlight—down on one knee. Swallowing hard, she turned Tillamook around, pulling on the reins tight until she stood on the outside of the proposal. Millie arrived just in time to hear Ray shout, "Hell, yes. It's about damn time, my love."

Dex, Gale and Ray all laughed as Gale swept up his husband-to-be and twirled him in the sand before planting him firmly on safe ground, his arm wrapped tight around Ray's waist until he was settled. When they kissed, Millie wiped at a tear she hadn't felt fall.

She clapped enthusiastically, whooping with congratulations.

"Hey, hun. Wasn't that romantic?" Dex asked her, riding up next to her. He leaned over and she met him halfway across the distance between their horses and their lips grazed.

"It was. Terribly." But that wasn't why her stomach still hadn't settled. Dex actually seemed to mean what he said, and not because they were within earshot of the happy couple.

"C'mon," Dex said, tossing her a smile that made

her knees as squishy as her stomach. "Let's give them some time alone."

"Hold up," Gale called out. He ran up to them, his breathless smile and bright eyes visible even in the pale moonlight. "We just want to thank you both."

"For what?" Millie asked.

"You gave me the courage to live my truth with Ray. Loving him has been an adventure, but until I talked to you both, saw how you work alongside each other with such ease and still keep the romance alive, I didn't think that would be possible for us."

Millie shot Dex a look, but he was just smiling at Gale, nodding along to the little speech.

"I'm glad you two are taking this leap. It's worth it, trust me," Dex said. Millie had to work against gravity and abject shock to keep her jaw from hitting the sand.

"Dex, I know we talked about it earlier, but are you still okay with me riding back with Ray and taking the rest of the night off?"

"To quote your fiancé, *hell yes*!" They both laughed while Millie kept a smile plastered to her face. It might have been a demonic clown smile, but it was all she was capable of as she watched Dex flippantly talk about marriage and romance. As far as she'd been aware, he considered both to be illnesses with only fatal outcomes. It's not like she'd disagreed with him, either. Until lately, anyway. But then…why hadn't he said anything to her about their future?

"Great. You two have fun and thanks for taking the patients back to the barn. You've got this weekend off to show our appreciation."

"Normally, I'd refuse politely, but I've got plans for this little lady, so we'll take it."

Gale jogged back to his fiancé and helped him back on his horse.

"We've got plans?" Millie asked, her brows raised in question.

"We do. Secret plans."

"So secret I can't know?"

"Yep. What good is making a surprise date for my wife, only to tell her about it?"

Millie glanced around as they meandered back toward the trail of patients. "You know it's just us, right? Everyone else is too far away to hear anything."

He cocked his head. "Yeah. So?"

So we're not actually married. You don't need to pretend.

"Nothing. Never mind."

He shrugged like this was all normal. It was *not*. Dex Shaw talking about proposals and love and other sappy stuff he usually avoided like it all came from the infectious disease wing? Yeah, she'd have bet on cigarettes making a comeback to cure asthma before Dex's sappy streak.

And yet, he'd still kept his feelings about her tight-lipped. She wasn't sure anymore what was the truth and what was fabricated for their positions.

"You don't feel the least bit guilty for what he said back there?"

Dex's brows furrowed and his trademark shrug looked almost comical in the blue tint of the evening.

"No, why?"

"For them giving us praise for showing them how a relationship can be. I don't want to be the one to shine a light on this, especially tonight, but—" she lowered her voice so it was nothing more than a whispered hiss "—*we're not actually married. We're just best friends who have good sex.*"

She held out her hands as if to say, *See?*

Was she imagining it, or when Dex pulled back on his reins, did she see hurt etched on his handsome, rugged features?

"That's all this is to you?"

"I didn't mean that. I just meant—"

"I know what you meant, but I disagree. I care about you and I like what we're doing. I thought we were more."

"More?" she asked, her voice sounding wounded and almost unrecognizable. She'd hoped to have "the talk" at some point with Dex, but here? Under these circumstances? It was less than ideal. "Dex, wait." He slowed, then paused before turning back to her. "I like you, too. A lot. In case you forgot, I'm the one who admitted that first. I'm just trying to navigate what's real and what's...fiction," she said.

He sighed and nodded as if he understood.

"I get it. And believe me, it's just as hard for me to tell you the way I feel—I found the DWB pamphlet, Millie."

"Oh."

"Yeah. It threw me. I want…something *bigger* with you but it's clear you're marching ahead, ever the good soldier."

"That's not fair. You haven't said anything about what you're doing after this contract and it's not like we've looked for something together. I was pretty clear what I'd need to do if I didn't find anything permanent here. It wasn't a state secret."

Not like the rest of her feelings. Or the entirety of their relationship.

"I know, and you're right. I just don't…" His jaw was set, worried. "I just don't know what to do." His voice was barely above a whisper.

She hedged her next words carefully. "Then why not—?" The rest of the words stuck in her throat. *Why not marry me for real? Let's give this a try!*

Yeah, that would be rich.

Their marriage would likely be as short as Dex's towel in the bunkhouse. Because even if she let DWB go, her life was filled with more adventure—more risk—than he would want. And she didn't see a life of being tied down. More things they'd both known when they started this affair. It hadn't stopped them from leaving their good sense at the door, anyway.

Good soldier, indeed.

Her heart thumped out a rhythm of longing for the man beside her. Was it loud enough for him to hear this time?

"What do you want?" she asked instead.

Another Dexter Shaw shrug greeted her by way of an answer.

Typical.

"I'm not sure," he said, finally.

"Me, neither," she replied.

"Would you be up for doing what we're doing and seeing where it goes the next couple months?"

Why? So this cut can slice deeper when we say goodbye later?

"Yes," she whispered instead. Then, "Sure. I like what we're doing."

The lie sat heavy on her heart, making the pale blue seem darker, more ominous than romantic.

She *didn't* like what she and Dex were doing. Not one bit. If it were up to her, he'd hitch a ride on her train and they'd travel the world together as a couple, building memories and a life together.

But she'd chosen the wrong man for that. Especially because the infinitesimal flutter in her chest had turned to a gentle roar that couldn't be quieted anymore. How she felt about Dex couldn't be clearer—or louder.

She *loved* him.

She loved him, and yet…she couldn't imagine changing her life and her dreams to be with him. So there she was, stuck in the middle of a tar field, unable to move in either direction. Though it was far too difficult to imagine walking away from him while they still had some time left to enjoy each other, the next months would pass in the blink of an eye.

Her heart swelled against her rib cage.

And it would be damn near impossible to leave him then.

CHAPTER TEN

A WEEK HAD passed since the romantic beach ride. When they got back to the bunkhouse after work, Millie collapsed on the bed. She kicked off her boots and unbuckled her belt, but that's where her energy petered out. She was three seconds from catatonic. When she yawned, her eyelids fought against gravity to open again. She could sleep in her jeans and flannel, right?

Yeah, if you want your sheets to smell like wet horse all week.

She pouted, her bottom lip stuck in a three-year-old-who-wants-ice-cream position. Her eyes caught a photo on the nightstand that hadn't been there earlier that day. It was a framed image of her laughing at something Dex had said—was it when he'd wondered aloud if Cambria had a dry cleaner?—and him gazing down at her with a warmth in his eyes, his arm around her shoulder.

Gale had taken it before she and Dex were actually together. She smiled.

"When did you print that?" she asked, gesturing to the frame.

He shrugged, classic Dex. "When I ran into town to get stuff from the pharmacy. I like that smile on your face, so I figured why not put it out so I can see it every day."

It was so simple a statement, but it had the force of a hurricane, spinning Millie's world around. They probably should print some photos of the past fifteen years and put them up, since they didn't have wedding photos or other mementos a real marriage would have.

"Well, I like it, too. Thanks."

"You bet. Wanna clean off with me?" he asked.

"I don't wanna shower. I'm exhausted, babe."

She cringed as the word *babe* came out of her mouth. They weren't lying anymore by saying how much they cared for each other, but she'd been lying to herself and Dex for a good week about her true feelings. She loved him. And not in a sham best-friend-posing-as-a-husband way. Somehow, the "faking it" had turned into something genuine and irreplaceable.

Too real.

He didn't seem to notice her slipup, though. He bent over her, planting a kiss on her forehead.

"You're gorgeous either way."

"I'm not worried about my looks, but thank you." Heat fanned her cheeks at his compliment. "I smell like the floor of a barn."

As much as she tried to hold his liquid gaze, the way his triceps flexed as he balanced above her pulled her focus. The heat on her skin spread south—way south, pooling in her stomach.

His pull on her was magnetic. Feral. Nothing phony about it.

He kissed her again, this time on the lips, his tongue teasing her open.

"Well," he whispered, his breath hot on her skin, "good thing I made arrangements so you don't have to shower."

"Are you bringing the wash stall hose in here?"

He shook his head, his eyes gleaming. "Nope. I'm bringing you to the wash stall."

Confusion spread from her furrowed brows to her pursed lips.

"If you hope to make it till tomorrow, you'd better be kidding."

He gave his quintessential Dexter shrug, but the smile tugging at the corners of his mouth said he was up to something.

"Come on. I'll show you."

"Dex," she whined, curling into a ball on top of the comforter. "I'm tired."

"I know." He held out his hand for her to take.

When had he ever steered her wrong? He might be a little intense when it came to her safety, but he always had her best interests at heart. She grabbed his hand and squealed as, in one swift movement, he hoisted her into his arms, cradling her like the toddler she was behaving as.

On the way out the door, he grabbed a bag she hadn't noticed perched at the base of their entryway.

"Where are we going?" she asked.

"Shh… Relax and trust me," he whispered. Her head rested against his chest, the *thump-thump* of his heartbeat matching pace with his steps, nudging her further toward sleep.

Trusting Dex was as easy as breathing. They

worked well together as medical professionals and partners, each complementing the other's strengths with their own.

The harder thing to do was relax into him. Physically, sure. That was a pleasure she took advantage of all too often. But emotionally? Their fairy tale still had an expiration date and no matter how much she loved him, she couldn't fully relax knowing that.

"What're you doing?" she asked when they showed up at the front door of Ray and Gale's cabin. Dex kept her in his arms, but procured a key from his pocket, using it to unlock the front door. "Dex, what are we doing here?" she hissed. "This is Ray and Gale's place."

"Yep." He smiled and shut the door behind them.

"Put me down, Dex. This is crazy. We can't be here."

"I kinda like carrying you over thresholds, wifey. And don't worry. They offered the place to us."

"Why would they do that? We have a cabin."

Her eyes darted around the room. Even though she was on edge, she couldn't help but notice their surroundings. This cabin was bathed in rustic chic, a Chip and Joanna–looking masterpiece. White-washed frames housed photos of the couple and other family members, fresh flowers graced the large oak dining table and a floating natural edge pine shelf above the fireplace made the place feel... like a *home*.

It triggered a vague memory of her stepmother—before the death of her father—putting roses from

KRISTINE LYNN 157

her garden in a pale green vase every Sunday night. The news came from the naval chaplains on a Sunday, and flowers never graced their table again. In a sense, Millie had lost both parents when her dad was killed in Kuwait. What filled the gaping hole her father's absence made was a deep desire to be like him. She was a preteen when he passed, but she recalled him as kind and loving, if a little quiet. Her stepmom, on the other hand, became a shell of the woman she'd been when Millie was a child, leaving Millie to raise herself on good days. On bad? The woman was abusive and cruel, blaming Millie for her misery. That is, until her stepmother became sick and all but demanded Millie stay to care for her.

Any semblance of a family or childhood was stripped from her, carving out a need that seemed impossible to fill most days. Lacking any other guidance, she'd followed in her dad's footsteps and joined the military, which covered her bachelor's degree. In his death, her father's service to his country had then paid for her medical school. The army medical corps gave her back a family, even if it was short-lived.

It was a good life by some accounts; a desperately lonely one by others.

An ache opened up in Millie's chest, releasing a longing that she'd kept locked away tight. This place—this *home*—made her crave more.

A home of her own. Love to fill it. A family that would come home to her...

Her breathing relaxed, but her pulse raced. She'd

been able to curb those desires by meeting others, but now, sexually satisfied with a man she actually cared for—the rest came crashing back into her.

"Because of this," he replied, setting her down. The rose-tinted bubble of her overactive imagination popped, leaving her stranded alone, back in reality. A reality where she was in love with her best friend, who abhorred the lifestyle that had fulfilled and sustained her when nothing and no one else had.

Grabbing her hand, he led her down a hallway to a large oak door. When he pushed it open, she gasped, forgetting all about what she didn't have. What she *did* have was a deep clawfoot tub filled with bubbles and lined with candles. More fresh-cut flowers from around the property lined the marble shelves around the tub. It was breathtaking.

"Is this for me?"

"Of course. I'm here if you need me for anything, but there's a bottle of wine in the chiller by the tub and you don't have to leave until the water gets cold."

"What if something happens to one of the patients?"

"I've got the pager and my cell. I'm on call. You rest."

"But how—*when*…?"

Dex chuckled. "I had a little help. From Ray and Gale for letting me borrow this, of course. And Opie for setting it up while we were on the ride."

Opie, the property manager, did have a soft spot for Millie and Dex.

Millie's hand rested on her chest. "Why?" she whispered.

"Because you deserve it. Do I need another reason?"

She shook her head and Dex wrapped his arms around her, drawing her into him. She breathed him in, marveling at how he didn't smell like he'd been riding horseback all day, but like sweat and pine instead. It was earthy, magnetic and wholly seductive. So was his uncharacteristic romantic gesture—he'd told her he wasn't capable of it, but this scene begged to differ.

Okay, she admitted. *Maybe his penchant for nice things isn't always a bad thing.*

"I'm not sure I want to get in…" she said, turning to face him.

"Oh…uh… That's fine. You don't have to. I just thought with as hard as you've been working, you haven't had time to—"

"Without you. Join me?"

The tub was more than big enough to wrap them both in its warmth.

A smile spread across Dex's face. Good grief, he was handsome. And for the time being, that smile was turned on her. What more could she want?

She ignored the injured voice putting up an argument for a love that went beyond the physical. There was too much risk in opening that door tonight, while her body was tired and her heart sore.

Right now was time for her to get something else she wanted.

Her husband.

Her brain didn't correct her with the "fake" part of that agreement, finally going along with whatever fantasy Millie needed tonight.

She held Dex's gaze as she undid each button on her flannel. She wasn't taking her time, but she wasn't in a rush, either. All she wanted was to enjoy this moment with Dex. She let her shirt fall to her feet, revealing a white lace halter bra. Choosing to keep that on for now, she undid her belt and jeans and slid them off.

Dex licked his lips when she sat on the edge of the tub in nothing but matching lace undergarments and pointed to him.

"Your turn," she said.

He followed her lead, unbuttoning his own flannel, revealing a glistening chest and torso that also just happened to look like a diagram of the perfect male specimen from medical school.

Dex added his shirt to the pile and went to unbutton his jeans, but Millie frowned and shook her head.

"No. That's my job." She crooked a finger to call him over.

He obliged and she pulled his pants down just far enough to spring his length free from his boxers. Both of them gasped at the same time.

She stroked him, marveling at the pleasure personified in front of her. Teasing the tip of him with her thumb, she tucked the moan he made in the back of her heart for later. Whatever came of their relationship, she made him happy *now*. Desire flashed through her, hot and instant.

Moving her hand to cup his base, she took the rest of him in her mouth, sucking and flicking the tip of him with her tongue. He tasted of brine and salt, and her heart welcomed the reminder of the sea on her tongue.

His hands fisted in her hair, pulling her closer to him as he groaned with rapture. She worked her mouth and hand over him until he stiffened and released inside her. When he'd calmed, she pulled his pants off each leg one at a time.

"I think we should clean up together," she said, her voice thick with lust for the naked man in front of her. She lifted her arms, wordlessly instructing him to remove the last two articles of clothing she wore. He made quick work of the lace, adding them to the denim and cotton detritus behind them.

"Goddamn, Millie, you're going to be the death of me." The smile on his face said he wouldn't mind leaving the world that way, though. She smiled and slid into the water, gesturing that he join her.

This man—in all his glory, with more than enough to satisfy her—may not actually be her husband, but he was hers for right now and she was going to make damn sure she enjoyed it while it lasted.

Dex felt Millie's breathing slow and deepen before a gentle buzz of a soft snore confirmed she'd fallen asleep in his arms. He inhaled her damp hair, which now smelled like flowers and vanilla thanks to Gale and Ray's assortment of lathers. The tub water was still warm enough that he could justify not disturbing her yet.

His arms pulled her tighter to him, the feeling that he couldn't get close enough to her constricting his chest. The problem with Millie—her only flaw, and his fatal one—was that he could only ever get so close.

But now, with her safe in his arms, warm water blanketing them under quiet, understated light, he could rest easy. Except for the small tickle of an idea bothering his calm thoughts.

What if I ask her to stay? it wondered. *What if I asked her to actually be my wife?*

He pressed his lips to her hair and closed his eyes tight against the fear that answered the question for him. If she said yes, and ever got hurt, it would destroy him. Sure, that was the risk when you loved someone—a glaring reason he hadn't let anyone in until Millie—but when he knew her as he did, it was almost a certainty.

He sighed. The only thing worse than watching her get hurt would be seeing her attempt to mold herself into a life that didn't fit her shape. Watching her shrink and change just so he could selfishly cling tight to his own desires would ruin them both. His heart seized.

There has to be a way you can love each other where both of you get what you want out of life, it pressed.

It was all he wanted—he was pretty damn sure of that now. But if there was a way, he hadn't found it yet. Not only wasn't time on his side, but if he tried and failed? He'd lose the only thing that had ever mattered to him.

Millie wasn't just his best friend, nor simply his lover. She represented what he wanted—a partner he could trust and love, and not bear to lose.

That's impossible, his brain argued. *Loss is a part of life.*

But the response was purely academic. Dex knew that; he just didn't care.

She shifted, slipping into the nook between his chest and shoulder. He moved a string of damp hair off her forehead and gazed down at her smooth skin. This woman had never worn makeup, never hid behind anything other than who she was. Her authenticity made his attempts at it possible. The lie, the one that claimed they were married, was the steepest untruth she'd ever lived and it was only possible because of the degree of truth behind it. They loved and cared about each other and had for a decade and a half.

How was he supposed to ask her to live a bigger lie—one where he pretended she was happy staying in one danger-free place, and she pretended she didn't want to sprint from a life of sameness, routine and safety?

That kind of loss—watching her die slowly from boredom—would be worse than seeing her get hurt.

A shrill whine accompanied a steady buzz of something hard and plastic on wood, invading the tranquility and pensiveness of the moment. Every muscle in Dex's body tensed and flexed.

"Dammit," he muttered as the shift woke her.

"Wow. I must've dozed off," she said, stretching against him. "What is that?"

"The pager and cell are going off at the same time. Sorry it woke you. I was supposed to be back at the cabin if they went off."

She twisted so their faces were only an inch apart. Her lips pressed against his and his groin ached to love her again.

"I'm glad you stayed. This is exactly what I needed." She kissed him once more, this time teasing his mouth open so he could explore her. Maybe they could ignore the persistent beep and howl of the outside world encroaching on their moment. Only a few seconds later, though, she pulled away. "Let me get dressed and meet you outside."

"Just stay here. I'll be back as soon as I'm done."

"I'd like to help."

"Let me see what's going on first. I'd prefer you rest and let me handle whatever's up."

She smiled and sat up so Dex could stand and exit the tub.

"It's too lonely in here without you."

Dex checked the pager. It was a panic attack in Reese's room. He could treat her alone so Millie could stay warm and relaxed. When he answered the call, though, that idea flew out the window.

"This is Dex."

"Hey, this is Opie. Sorry to bug you, but we've got a situation."

"What's going on?" Dex asked, skipping pleasantries. Opie never called unless he had to. Millie stood up and leaned in, listening. Dex traced her dripping, naked silhouette with his eyes, his hands itching to join.

"Kelly Price sliced her leg on the edge of the bunkhouse coffee table and her roommate saw the blood. She's not doing so hot, Doc."

"Kelly or Reese?"

"Kelly's fine, but the gash is pretty deep—probably needs to be sewn up. I already fixed the chipped part of the table so it won't happen again."

"Good thinking, Opie. And Reese?" he asked. He was already using his free hand to towel off and his heart sank when Millie followed suit. When she held up her lace underwear, he nodded. He'd need her help, like it or not.

"She's curled up in a ball, shivering even though the heat's turned up in that bunkhouse hot enough to bake cookies on the windowsill. I ain't never seen anything like it, even here."

"It's an acute panic attack," Dex said, shimmying on his jeans. "She'll be okay, but we need to get there fast. Do me a favor, Opie."

"You bet."

"Move all the residents to the male cabin for now and help them set up the cots we have out for family weekend. I'd like to not move Reese if I don't have to."

They hung up, each with tasks to check off. Dex's were simple. Get dressed, kiss Millie and apologize for ruining the calm he'd promised, then sprint to the female bunkhouse. He packed a clonazepam in case Reese was still in active panic but hoped he wouldn't have to use it. Millie had told him Reese was trying to manage her symptoms medication-free since her biological father was an addict.

"I'll grab my suture kit and meet you there," Millie said, already dressed with her hair tied back in a braid. She kissed him before he got the chance. "And before you even think about apologizing, don't. This is the kind of stuff I took the job for. I'm happy to help."

He only nodded, a thread of his feelings for her from earlier tugging at his heart. The woman always seemed to surprise him, but that shouldn't have been much of a shock anymore. She was amazing. End of story.

He'd just have to wait until all their crises were behind them to decide what he'd do about that.

When they were both dressed and the cabin was locked back up, they jogged over to the women's bunkhouse behind the small apartment they shared. Dex knocked just in case, and Opie opened the door.

"Glad you're here, Doc. It's gettin' worse."

"Thanks, Opie. We've got it from here, but you did good tonight."

The man blushed a warm pink that made him look younger than his mid-seventies.

"I've got Reese if you can suture Kelly's leg," Dex told Millie quietly.

"Sure, but then I'd like to join you with Reese. I've seen a lot of the same things she has and we've built a strong relationship."

"Sounds good."

Dex slowed his pace so he didn't frighten Reese

or trigger her panic attack. He put his hands in his pockets, tracing the edge of the pill packet as he approached Reese.

His heart lurched at the sight of her crumpled body, pressed as tight against the corner of the cabin as she could be. Her personality was one of the more infectious of the patients at Hearts and Horses; she could always be counted on to crack a joke just when it was needed. The way she hummed when she walked places had earned the nickname Happy Feet for her.

But like this? Compact and shivering on the cold wood floor? It was soul-crushing.

Take a deep breath and be there for her.

Confidence filled the space in his chest carved out by seeing his patient in pain. He'd done good work and made time to heal himself in the process. Even the hints of darkness each time Millie had gotten hurt had stayed put.

Sure. It has nothing to do with that same woman screwing you into fake wedded bliss.

Ignoring the less than helpful snark his subconscious drummed up, Dex kneeled next to Reese. He brushed the skin on the inside of her wrist and though her eyes darted toward him, they went back to the invisible spot she focused on in the distance almost immediately. Since she didn't flinch, he rested two fingers on her pulse and took note of the elevated heart rate.

"Reese, it's me, Dr. Shaw. Can you look at me?"

She did, briefly, then her bottom lip quivered, her eyes watered and she looked away again.

"Your pulse is a little too high for my comfort. I'd like to give you a small dose of clonazepam to settle your blood pressure and make it a little easier to come down from this. What do you say?"

It was his ace in the hole, telling her his plan. Hopefully it would rouse her enough for him to talk her off the knife's edge of panic she rested on.

"No," she said. Her voice was rough but quiet. "I—I don't want medication."

"Okay. That's fair." He breathed out a sigh of relief. He didn't want to have to medicate her, especially when it was against her own vision of her long-term treatment. But if she'd remained unresponsive, he wouldn't have had a choice. "Do you mind telling me what happened?"

Reese's eyes focused, leaving only a faint hint at the trauma brewing beneath her exterior. This was a hardened police officer meeting his gaze, a woman used to walking up to her breaking point, staring it in the face and standing tall against the pressure to cave in.

"I lost it. It's not like it's even a bad gash," she said. But the subtle shiver that rolled through her told Dex she didn't fully believe that. "And it's not like I haven't seen worse. I was in downtown LA, for eff's sake."

Dex chuckled and the corner of Reese's lips twitched up. She was going to be okay. This was a scare, but one she'd recover from.

"Yeah, but you know darn well healing isn't linear."

"Your wife said the same thing," Reese said.

"I wish I was strong like her, that blood didn't bother me."

"She's a smart, strong woman to be sure. You are, too, though."

"I—I don't feel like it right now. I couldn't get myself to stop imagining Urie—my partner—on the ground. He was shot saving me."

"I'm so sorry to hear that. But you did talk yourself down. You refused medication, and that's a huge step, Reese."

A blush of red splashed her cheeks. "It is?"

"Very much so. So what would you like to do? You're the expert of your own life, Reese. I'm just here to help."

Her shoulders rolled back, her jaw set with confidence.

"Can you help me get to bed? I'm cold and exhausted."

Dex helped her into her cot and glanced at the partition where Millie worked on her patient while he made sure Reese was comfortable.

Your wife.

The words no longer sent a ripple of fear through him when he heard them. Instead, a warm flush of something else spread from his chest outward.

Pride.

He liked the sound of Millie as his wife. More than that, he liked the *feel* of it.

From their vantage point, he couldn't see Kelly, but Millie was in view, her gaze pinned to where Kelly's face must be. Her voice was calm—a healing cadence and tone he recognized as her "doctor's voice."

She's so good at this.

Her laughter at something Kelly said rippled through the air, hitting him square across the chest. He loved this woman, and always had.

Fine. But could you let her loose into the world to pursue the dangerous career choices she craves? Because if not, you're setting yourself up for disappointment. Her, too.

He knew that. And he could. Because it wasn't so bad, the worrying-about-her thing. As it turned out, there was something worse than that—imagining her doing all that and never knowing how it went, or what amazing feats she accomplished.

Well, hell.

Was he really thinking about committing to someone and risking the chance that, one way or another, he might lose her?

I am.

The only remaining question was when to tell her how he felt. Because if he told her and they really did this, he couldn't walk away.

Dex was inclined to be careful, but for the first time in his life, being cautious was the last thing he wanted. It was time to be bold and brave like the woman he loved.

CHAPTER ELEVEN

ON THE FRIDAY of Family Weekend, the ranch was abuzz. The twenty-two patients were outside, cleaning the grounds in lieu of a late morning group session, and all the talk Millie passed expressed excitement over who was coming to visit and what the patient couldn't wait to share about their camp experience.

"I think my son's favorite will be Lightning, same as mine," Charlie said.

"Yeah, no way my wife is going near the stables, but she'll like the wine tasting we have on the last night."

Millie smiled. That was a nice little perk Millie had proposed to Gale.

When she walked behind Reese, Millie caught a snippet of her conversation, too.

"My mom loves horses, but I really can't wait to introduce her to Dr. Tyler-Shaw. That woman is one of the only reasons I'm ready to see my folks again."

"Same here," Peters, a former airman, said.

Millie beamed. She was doing good work. Work that mattered.

Doctors Without Borders does good work, too.

Without another full-time option to follow this contract, it was the only one in front of her.

We could always ask to stay here.

Yeah, if you tell Ray and Gale the truth about who you are.

That was more difficult than imagining sticking around and working here with Dex indefinitely. The lie had spun out of control... The thing was, it was closer to the truth now, though; she and Dex were together, and lately, she couldn't recall the impetus of her drive to travel, to ship herself off to foreign countries, some of which didn't approve of a female physician.

She hoped it was because her dreams had shifted, not because of Dex. She *couldn't* be the kind of woman who sacrificed her dreams for a guy.

Not even a man she'd cared for her entire adult life.

Not even a man who knew just how to use his lips to make her toes curl with desire.

Except...

When that man walked by her, deep in conversation with Gale, he winked at her and her body flat out didn't get the memo. As always happened when he flirted with her, her knees went weak and her heart thumped against her chest, wildly trying to get her attention.

Let him do that thing with his tongue and you'll forget all about DWB.

She frowned until he circled back around and kissed her cheek. She flushed, heat spreading out and down from the spot his lips touched.

I get it, she told her heart. *We work when it comes to* that. *But what about the rest?*

"How's your day going, beautiful?"

The flush deepened and she fanned her cheeks. At least he couldn't read the not-so-innocent thoughts racing through her head.

"Good." She busied herself picking weeds around the entrance sign so she wouldn't be tempted to shuck this whole cleanup and take Dex behind the barn for a literal roll in the hay. "I'm excited to meet the families and for them to see the progress their loved ones are making."

"It'll be a good weekend for sure. I'm a little worried about new riders on the horses, if I'm being honest, though."

"I hear you, but it's pretty cute that you're calling other people new riders now," she teased, dumping her handful of weeds in the compost. He chuckled and his eyes danced with a spirit she hadn't seen in them in all the years she'd known him.

"Well, I'm three and a half months into my new professional riding career, so I can hardly call myself a novice anymore. I mean, I'm surprised they're not calling me up to stunt ride for *Yellowstone*."

Millie laughed, sobering only when his arms wrapped around her waist. She still wasn't used to the whole PDA thing with a man she'd loved from afar for so long. Somewhere along the line, they'd taken their fake-marriage-but-real-dating thing out of their cabin, and no one seemed the wiser. What did it say that their now real romance was believable enough to think the two were newlyweds?

Would it be so different outside the ranch?

It will if I try something outside his comfort zone and he flips out. What will I do then? I won't shrink for any man, not even Dex.

"Your time's coming, I'm sure. Anyway, Ray is a rockstar and won't let anything happen to any of the guests."

"You're right, as usual," Dex said, planting a soft kiss on her lips.

"I could get used to that," Millie said, meeting his gaze.

"Well, then come here and let me do it again," he said, pulling her in.

She backed away and smiled. "I meant you telling me I'm right."

Dex laughed, his head tossed back. With his hair grown out long and his beard filled in, he was starting to look the part of a cowboy. His shirt was wrinkled along the sleeves and he didn't seem to care. He'd tucked away his clothing iron under the bed and even stopped using hair gel a couple weeks ago. Someone else might think he'd all but given up, but Millie saw it as a sign of growth. He was letting go of his need to control every situation.

She was growing, too. Letting Dex into her bed was one thing, but she'd opened up and told him more about her stepmother, too.

Only a small worry nagged at her when she remembered what their arrangement was. He still hadn't asked her to stay, or looked for jobs with her. If she asked Ray and Gale to stay, it would be just for herself unless she and Dex had a talk and ironed things out.

Nerves tickled her skin.

If they talked, and it didn't go the way she hoped, she'd lose Dex as both her fake husband and her best friend. Things were fine as they were—why mess with them?

"Oh, honey, we've got a lifetime of you being right and me just hanging on for the ride."

He grabbed her hand and any unease about their future slipped away through their palms like sand. His words washed over her like a balm.

We've got a lifetime...

Were they just words spoken for the benefit of the staff and patients walking around them? Or was Dex hinting at something more? The back and forth of wondering what to do with her growing feelings was bugging her.

"Hey, you two lovebirds. When you get a sec, I'd love to steal Millie for a debrief."

Millie pulled out of Dex's hand, the space Dex had just occupied empty and cold.

"But of course, Ray. I'm just saying goodbye to this guy since he's on second shift."

She and Dex were trading off the first day so there was someone always on call in case the patients needed it when their families arrived.

"Bye, babe," she said, reaching up on her toes to kiss him perfunctorily.

He nuzzled her neck, then whispered, "Bye, love," before winking and walking away.

Love? He'd never called her that before. *Tyler,* yes. *Millie,* more often of late. But *love?*

Dizziness swirled around her. So many clues

were stacking against her heart, but if she was misreading the signs, if Dex was just playing the game, they'd topple and her heart might break. Why couldn't things have just stayed as they were—best friends sleeping together and faking a marriage?

A real relationship was much trickier and even though she enjoyed the perks, she wasn't sure she appreciated the discomfort.

"You two are almost too adorable for words," Ray said as they walked toward the main barn.

Millie forced a smile as she shoved her overactive thoughts to the back of her mind.

"Coming from you, that's a compliment."

"We're happy, Mil."

She gazed over at her friend and colleague and grinned at Ray's sudden change in tone.

"I can tell. But you're worried?" she guessed.

He nodded. "What if this isn't what he wants in the end? I mean, I come with a lot of baggage," he said, gesturing to his leg and arm.

"No," Millie disagreed. "You don't. Not physically, anyway—your injuries are part of your story, but they aren't baggage. Now, your penchant for reality TV?" she teased. "That's some hefty emotional baggage, but," she said, growing serious again, "it's up to our partners to decide what they're willing to carry. And Gale made his choice."

Millie let that settle on her shoulders as they entered the barn. Ray had just given a name to the slinking, pervasive fear lingering just below each kiss, each embrace from Dex. When would it get to be too much for him? When would she do something that triggered his past memories of being abandoned?

"All we can control is what we do and how we show up. You know darn well we can't pin our hopes on what-ifs so we shouldn't let them hold up our fears, either," she said, as much to herself as to Ray.

"And that's why you're my favorite therapist-slash-friend."

"Don't you forget it," she joked back. They joined the rest of the first crew on deck for the arrival of the families in a couple hours.

"Okay, now that we're all here, let's talk about a game plan for emergencies as well as who will be where for the arrival." Gale had a clipboard out, a pen in his other hand and a whistle around his neck. He looked like a cross between a camp counselor and a serious cowboy.

"Look at my man, all serious and organized. God, he's never been hotter," Ray whispered. He winked and Millie snorted back a laugh.

Gale's brows rose a good two inches.

"You're gonna get me in so much trouble," she hissed.

"Not as much trouble as my fiancé is gonna be in. I have big plans for that whistle later. The clip-board, too."

Millie barely masked the laugh that rose in her chest as a cough. When the fit of giggles subsided, what replaced it almost knocked Millie on her backside. It was guilt, hot and acidic. But…*why*?

A glance at Ray confirmed her worries.

You feel guilty about lying to them.

Sure, she always had, but it was worse now that they considered each other friends and not just colleagues. All she wanted was to dump her woes at Ray's feet the same way he'd trusted her, but if she did, he'd know the truth—that the thin veil of authenticity about her and Dex was a result of their employment as physicians at Hearts and Horses, not the precursor.

And then what? Would Ray and Gale—and the patients—ever forgive them?

Just get through the next few months. Then you'll be off on another adventure and Dex will be...wherever he is. It's the bright side of this short contract.

But that didn't sit well, either.

Because she didn't want a short contract; she wanted to stick around at a place closer to home that needed dedicated trauma doctors and psychologists like her and Dex. A place like Hearts and Horses.

"Hey, Ray," she whispered while Gale walked around to give everyone their assignments, "can I talk to you later?"

"Sure." He turned to face her. "Is everything okay?"

She nodded, regretting speaking up at all. It wasn't fair to spill her guts to him without running it by Dex first, since it was his job and friendships on the line, too.

She made her lips twist into a smile. "Yeah. Perfect. Hey, I'm gonna run and check on Reese before we gear up. You good here?"

He nodded and Millie left the barn, the half lie about where she was headed adding to the pile of mistruths at her feet. She wanted to come clean, to tell Ray and Gale and beg for forgiveness if need be, but first she had to clear a few things up.

First on the list was arguably the hardest. She had to ask Dex what all his dropped clues meant, the risks of it going awry be damned. Regardless of his answer, she needed to tell him how she felt about him, the *L* word thick on her heart and tongue. If he didn't want more from her, the lies piling up around them were the least of her concerns.

Picking up the shattered pieces of her heart would most certainly top the list then.

But that could only happen after she met with her patient, meaning she had to push back the talk she'd asked Dex for, too.

Great, she thought as she wound through the camp to where Dex was helping with the last of the cleanup. *So much for looking forward to a relaxing weekend.*

Dex whistled along the dirt road leading up to the entrance of Hearts and Horses. Just a few short months ago, he and Millie had arrived through those gates with a fabricated story and hidden traumas.

God, had it really only been a few months? It felt more like a lifetime with all that had changed. Not just his feelings for Millie, though having those out in the open and reciprocated—most of them, anyway—was enough to make a man believe in the kind of healing he practiced on others.

No. *He* was different, down to his core. Calm, the kind he'd worked to get his patients to experience, rolled through him. His panic attacks were almost a thing of the past. And darn if he wasn't getting accustomed to loving Millie's little quirks, including the edge she rode between danger and fun. That was *her*, and loving her meant loving *all* of her, or at least he thought so.

Only a shred of doubt remained regarding their future, but that was normal, right?

Okay, so maybe their future—where they'd live, where they'd work, did they want a formal marriage, and perhaps kids?—was bigger than it seemed, but they'd made such amazing progress so far. What lay ahead had to be easier than the path it'd taken them to get here, right?

All that was left was to tell the woman. And he had a plan for that, one that would give him a chance to show off his romantic streak of late. It was also, hopefully, foolproof so it minimized the risks of her turning him down and taking with her the best thing that had ever happened to him.

"Speaking of the she-devil," he called out when she strode around the corner. Her curls blew behind her in the breeze and she tilted her head, smiling the bright toothy smile that had first wormed its way into his heart fifteen years ago.

"Not sure I love that nickname, but I'm glad to know you were talking about me." She glanced around and her smile fell. "But…to whom?"

He laughed. "Myself. I had some minor convincing to do before you and I connected tonight."

"Uh-oh. Do I like the sound of that?"

"I hope you do." The lunch bell chimed at the barn and Dex cursed it under his breath. Doubts or not, he was going to tell Millie he loved her. The magnitude of that one little statement, the three shortest words he'd ever said, both weighed on him and lifted him up. Hell, they'd been bubbling around in his chest for fifteen years, even if they sounded different to him back then. "But…duty calls right now."

"Actually, I was hoping we could move our talk?"

"Now *I'm* worried. What's up?"

She smiled, which curbed the bottoming out of his stomach. With her hands shoved deep in her pockets, she tilted up on her toes and planted a kiss on his cheek. She smelled sweet and salty at the same time. Like the Pacific Ocean breeze had kissed a caramel candy before settling on the nape of her neck.

They held hands on the short walk to lunch. Could she feel the heat building between their skin every time they touched? She had to—it was too intense to ignore. He didn't take for granted how new this ability was, to love her so openly in front of everyone they knew.

"I promised I'd take Reese's family to the local beach that Gale showed us that first week so they can see the stars out here, and you've got that night shift. Can I get a rain check for after the ride tomorrow? I think we both have an hour off before lunch."

"Sure. Yeah, sounds great." The idea of waiting any longer to put his plan into action was excruciating, but what choice did he have? He kissed the edge of her lips and Millie's cheeks turned the shade of pink that made her look caught in a windstorm. With her wild curls and moisture-lined eyes that belied a storm beneath her calm exterior, she painted a pretty picture of what getting lost in her tempest would be like.

"Thanks. See you, cowboy," she said. She jogged ahead to a waving Reese without looking back and the doubt pulsed in his chest. It was a huge risk, telling her he loved her. More than not having a home to go back to at night. If he gave her his heart, it could be left out in the cold or hanging over a cliff and he couldn't very well ask for it back, could he?

Cheese and rice.

This is why he'd never let his feelings see the light of day until now. They didn't know how to behave.

After lunch, he headed to finish cleaning up the common areas. The barn was next, a chore he definitely didn't mind anymore. Horses were, as it turned out, kinda cool. And it didn't hurt that the rides with patients helped his job immensely.

Sure, that was the point of equine therapy, but in LA, even in a progressive hospital like Mercy, there wasn't a lot of stock given to alternative treatments for mental health. Physical, sure—every juice bar, Pilates or yoga studio, and gym cluttering up downtown said as much. But for mental health? It was exercise, meditate and make weekly pilgrimages to a therapist, or medicate.

Horses—all animals, actually—were a new treatment protocol for Dex and it suited him. The danger of putting a patient challenged with PTSD on the back of a half-ton animal even seemed normal by now.

If only that—the horses, the excitement on the patients' faces as they took their family on a tour of the facilities they'd called home the past few months, even the knowledge that he was doing damn good work that was making a difference in people's lives—could hold his focus.

All he could think about was Millie as he mucked stalls, shined equipment and introduced himself to the loved ones of his patients. Every second he couldn't tell her how he felt was another moment the shred of doubt grew. Especially as he watched her jump on the back of a moving four-wheeler, then come back riding the new horse bareback as she prepped for the big ride coming up.

The doubt swirled with fear.

He'd thought he nipped both, but there they were, ugly and pervasive.

"A penny for your thoughts?" Gale asked, and Dex tried on a relaxed smile. Like the rest of his mannerisms that afternoon, though, it fell flat. He closed out of the check-in email with the family members' names he was still attempting to commit to memory. "Oh, I see. A dollar, then? Looks like you've got the weight of the world on your shoulders this morning."

"Just the North American continent," Dex joked.

"Wanna talk about it?"

Dex froze. He did. And Gale had become a close enough confidant that he was just the sort of person he'd like to unpack his feelings with. No, that wasn't true. Gale wasn't just a confidant… He was a *friend*.

And Dex couldn't tell his friend what sat heavy on his heart because he'd been straight up lying to the guy since the start. He couldn't really just come out and say, "Well, actually, I'm in love with the woman posing as my wife and I'd like to ask her to be in a real committed relationship, but I'm afraid of what that'll do to my insecurities about being abandoned. I'm also afraid of loving a woman so bent on living on the edge when that kind of life makes me feel unsafe. More than any of that, I kinda want to stay. Here. So, what do you think I should do?"

"I'm just wondering what to do next. I think Millie would like to head off on some adventure in a place where she can help patients who don't have access to good care…" Dex drifted off, the truth of his admission buoying the weight of his guilt ever so slightly.

"And you don't want that kind of danger, that kind of risk?" Gale asked. He handed Dex a diet soda.

"Thanks," Dex said. Gale had nailed his feelings, even working with a limited scope of knowledge.

"And yeah, that pretty much sums it up. How'd you know?"

Gale laughed heartily. "Because you're the mirror image of Ray and me."

"Really?" It shouldn't make him feel better to know he wasn't alone in his feelings, but it did.

"Yep. Every month or so, Ray gets a wild hair up his ass and wants to upend the life we've built here. I don't blame him. It's who he is. But it doesn't sit well with me. I'm a creature of comfort."

"Yeah." Dex gave Gale a half smile. "Me, too."

"And there isn't anything wrong with that."

"No, there isn't." Dex thought of his time living under the bridge. As if he had another choice other than seeking creature comforts after that.

"But there's also nothing wrong with the loves of our lives—bless their hearts—being a bit on the wilder side."

Dex's smile turned sour.

"I agree, but it isn't the easiest to live with."

"That's no joke." Gale looked off toward the entrance, where Ray was laughing with a patient's mother, his head tilted back. "But maybe there's another perspective."

"What's that?" At this point, Dex would take anything. Because he loved Millie. Loved her as much as he'd ever loved anything, really. But he still wasn't sure how to live with her, at least not in the long term.

"Millie and Ray are special. They see the world on their terms, not through the lens the world made for them. And that kind of special—the kind that shows up with a bouquet of wildflowers, a horse and a prepacked picnic at the bluffs? It grows you into the person you're meant to be." He inhaled, closed his eyes, and smiled. "And damn if that isn't the most frustrating part of it all."

"What's that?" Dex asked. He was following Gale up to that point.

"That they were right all along. Life's better with a little risk."

Dex sighed like he'd been waiting for that line to let him release what'd been stuck in his chest for months. Years, actually. He opened his mouth to offer a rebuttal—risk was inherently unsafe, though. And with his childhood, he needed safety, caution, security. But not more than he needed Millie; that much he'd decided. Even if he didn't know fully how to rectify the two.

There was a truth in Gale's words that hammered against his chest. Going to medical school, his residency at Stanford, then working at a premier hospital like Mercy—none of it had let him settle into his life, relax. If anything, it led to a different kind of anxiety. The kind that pressed against his back, shoving him forward, forward, forward at all costs.

Until Millie.

She'd not only awoken him to the possibilities he'd previously considered off the table, but Gale was right; they came with a serenity that he'd never felt, not one day in his life until now.

He…he wanted to be here, in Cambria. With Millie.

"Thanks, Gale."

Something else hung on Dex's neck, heavy and hot. *I have something to tell you*, it pulsed. But Dex couldn't get the words out.

"Don't mention it. I'm gonna go check in with our paramours, but you take your time."

He nodded, even though he didn't agree. He'd *been* taking his time. The wasted hours, days, months and years were at his back now, insistent that he not squander another damned minute.

But there was something else there, too. *Guilt*. For lying to Gale and Ray, and for what that meant—not just for him, but for Millie, too. She was the most honest person he knew so this must be eating her alive.

Sure, in the beginning, it'd seemed necessary, but now that they'd befriended their bosses? It stunk of duplicitousness. His skin itched and his chest burned when he couldn't take in deep enough breaths. The edges of anxiety slunk in amongst the fear and doubt.

One, two, three, he tried.

He breathed through it, but the fact that he hadn't gotten over near-attacks like that bothered him.

How was he supposed to be there for Millie if he couldn't handle his own messes?

But Millie wouldn't rely on him. Hell, that's why he loved her—she could handle her own stuff and they'd just be good partners. Still, no matter how they felt about each other—and he hoped they felt the same—they couldn't move forward like this. They had to tell Ray and Gale the truth and risk the consequences.

If they didn't come clean, the future he saw ahead of them wasn't ever going to happen. But if they were honest, it might not, either.

Damn, he thought. That was the problem with caring for someone—if it went wrong, it sure hung you out to dry, didn't it?

CHAPTER TWELVE

THE FAMILIES' EXCITEMENT down at the stables was palpable. Delight over the horses was matched only by George's preteen boys' joy over finding a pair of barn kittens. The boys pet the kittens, their voices a full octave higher than when they'd strode into the barn attempting to look tough enough to rival Ray and Gale's stoic cowboy stares.

Millie smiled. There was hope for the future generation, no matter what the pundits said. In her previous line of work, she'd almost lost sight of that, but here, optimism shone from some pretty dark places.

"I wonder if Dad will let us get some cats when he comes home," the taller of the two, Ben, said. He was the one challenged with autism, Millie knew, but out here, among the horses and miles of fresh air, even she had a hard time picking up on the stimming. Only his excessive blinking gave him away. Another win for equine therapy.

"No way. You know how he feels about animals in the house."

Millie pretended to watch a young girl pet Tillamook as George Dominic strode over to his sons.

"I heard you talking about those kittens. They're a lot of work, you know."

Ben nodded, a hesitant smile on his face. Millie stifled a laugh when his brother, Lance, rolled his eyes.

"Told you so," Lance muttered.

"But if you're willing to take it on, I reckon you're ready for the responsibility."

Millie couldn't keep the smile from her face. George had come a long way to accept that level of change, risk and uncertainty into his life. Pets didn't always follow the rules of a human who craved control, like George had been when he'd arrived at Hearts and Horses. Cats especially.

Who needed to travel to exotic locales to work when she could help people who needed it here— first responders like George, who did their jobs bravely, only to lose part of themselves in the process? Her help had a direct effect on more than just the patients. It saved families.

Millie glanced at Dex, who was showing Charlie's teen son how to saddle his horse. Would he ever accept the quandary that came with loving Millie, a woman filled to the brim with risk and uncertainty? Only time would tell. And time wasn't necessarily on their side. Not just because their contract was more than half over, but because of a single sheet of paper Ray had given her that morning sitting heavy in her back pocket—and on her heart.

She'd read it with interest, but how could she respond when she wasn't an "I" anymore? Being part of a "we" meant talking to Dex was necessary, especially since the paper had his name on it as well.

Needless to say, their long overdue conversation after the ride was even more necessary.

Millie focused on readying Tillamook while Gale issued instructions for what was coming up that morning. The ride would have the families paired with a staff member from the stables, Millie and Dex acting as roaming medical sentries, keeping an eye on the health of their patients. Gale didn't say as much out loud, but at the slightest nod from Millie or Dex, he would find an excuse—the weather, lame horse or something similar—and shut the event down.

The horses were part of the medical practice at Hearts and Horses, but they could be a liability when new variables were introduced. A tickle of nerves flitted through Millie's chest, but she tampered it. They were professionals.

"Hey there, beautiful," a velvety deep voice said from behind her. The worry turned to lust, hot and quick against her skin. She'd never get sick of hearing Dex's voice directed at her. Especially when he called her *beautiful*.

"Hi," she said. "How's your morning been?"

"Great, since I woke up in the middle of the night to a gorgeous woman curled up against my chest. Did you have fun last night?"

"I did. Reese cracks me up. We had a good talk, checked her levels of cortisone, then watched some reality TV."

Dex pretended to gag. "Better you than me."

"There's nothing I could do to convince you to watch baking shows with me?" she asked, trailing a finger along his chest, until it hooked his chin and brought his mouth to hers for a fiery kiss.

When she pulled away, he looked stunned. And happy.

"Okay, fine. Maybe a season or two if you keep that up."

Millie laughed, but it came out half-full.

His brows fell into a deep vee. "Is everything okay?"

Millie nodded, taking his hand in hers. "It is," she assured him. "With us, anyway."

"Okay," Dex conceded, though his eyes were still hard under furrowed brows. "We're still talking after the ride?"

"Yep."

"Then I'm looking forward to it."

His words didn't match his demeanor, though. He kissed her cheek, then walked toward the barn entrance, but not before glancing back at her twice. She sighed. If they weren't surrounded by people they cared for and needed to care for, she'd come right out and tell him. She didn't want to lie to Gale and Ray anymore.

And—this was the big one—she wasn't sure she wanted to travel for work anymore.

Not because of Dex, or at least not just because of him. The offer Ray made her that morning—an official contract folded in her jeans—fluttered in her rib cage like a bird in flight.

Stay on, he'd urged her. *Stay on and run a trauma program. If you do, and you can convince your husband to work on building a clinical therapy program, we can expand twofold, at least.*

The salary he'd offered on behalf of Hearts and

Horses was absolutely competitive, but that wasn't the real reason she was considering it. Damn if she didn't feel like she had a family for the first time in a long time. What she'd found—trust, companionship, honesty...*love*? It was more than she deserved but was quickly becoming impossible to live without.

Maybe—this was the part Ray had offered that meant more than the offer—she'd always run from job to job, looking for what she lacked from her family. That information sat square on her chest until her heart had cried uncle.

Ray was right.

If she wanted the love and support Ray and Gale gave her, she had to earn that in return.

But then...what would Dex think of that development? Would he be okay with coming clean, even if it meant they lost the deal on the table?

Her biggest fear, though, was that he'd feel an immense pressure on himself if she stayed in the US, whether or not she was doing it for him. This relationship worked because of who they were to each other. If she asked more of him than he was ready to give...

She gulped back a wave of nausea.

"You ready, Dr. Tyler-Shaw?" Gale called back from the front of the stables. The riders were all on horses and she was taking the first stint at the back of the pack.

"Sure am," she shouted, mustering a smile wide enough to let in a horse fly.

"All right, riders. Stay between Dr. Tyler-Shaw and myself and let's go have some fun."

As the riders left the barn one by one, Millie watched Dex at the middle of the pack. He was strong on top of his horse, confident and able in a way he hadn't been when he'd arrived. It looked good on him.

But good enough that he'd want a life of practicing this kind of medicine every day? With no cities, no nice restaurants, no clothes tailor-made to fit his impressive frame? To him, it was a life of adventure and wholly outside the comfort zone he resided safely within.

He did this for me, for the favor I called in.

And Dex made the most of everything, no matter what. Maybe this worked because it was temporary.

The air—cool with a hint of fall on its breath—was an intoxicating blend of woodfire and briny sea breeze. The scent tickled Millie's nostrils and reminded her to stay present in the moment. The future wasn't guaranteed one way or another, but this ride, this time in nature with patients she'd come to care about as much as for was.

"Good job, Tilly," she praised her horse as the gentle giant carried them up a steep embankment. It was the toughest part of the trail, especially for new riders, but everyone did great.

Okay. They'd made it through the hard stuff. Time to relax. The patients and their families laughed and talked and pet their horses, seeming to enjoy this part of their weekend.

Good. Horses were integral to their therapy now,

but this weekend signified a shift of responsibility to the patients' families to take over some of that, while the rest of the onus fell to the patients themselves.

"This is pretty great, isn't it?" Dex asked, sliding up next to her. They were stopped at the top of the ridge for one of George's boys to use nature's facilities.

"It is. I'm glad it's going well. For everyone's sake."

"How about you? You looked like you had something on your mind back there."

"Not here," she whispered.

"Why not?"

Oh, Dex.

If there was one thing Dex liked to see coming, it was anything that might throw his world off its axis. They had a rare moment together while Gale explained the history of the property and how Hearts and Horses came to be.

She exhaled, then took a deep slow breath. "I want to come clean about our...relationship."

He smiled and relief washed through her. "I agree. I wanted to ask for the same thing this afternoon. I can't stand lying to our friends."

"Exactly." She breathed a sigh of relief as large as the ocean looming in front of them. "And you're okay if they fire us on the spot? Because..." She pulled the sheet of paper from her pocket. "They offered us a full-time place here."

"Whoa. Then I guess we have to tell them. We can't keep this up forever."

Forever.

Warmth washed over her. This was going better than she thought it would. Dex had an aversion to risk, and their jobs on the line would definitely qualify. Would that translate to the other thing she had to tell him?

"I think we need to talk about the offer, but I agree about the other part. We need to tell them," he said.

"Okay, then, so it's settled."

"If we weren't on thousand-pound beasts right now, I'd hug you."

Millie's heart slammed against her chest. "You're happy about the contract?"

"I am. Holy hell, I hate worrying about you when you go to places that want to kill you. Are you thinking you'll take it?"

"Um, yeah." *You.* Not *we.* Her heart missed a beat.

"Awesome. You'll be safe, and I'll be happy." George called back to Dex something about his son's horse. Dex needed to concentrate—they had patients who needed them. "Anyway, let's talk more after the ride, okay, Tyler?"

Millie nodded, but Dex didn't see it since he rode off in service of his patient. Any delight she'd felt when Dex seemed pleased about her consideration of the full-time job was lost in the response he'd given her.

I'll be safe, so he'll be happy.

And he'd called her Tyler again. Like they were back to being good buds and nothing more.

Nothing about how they could be together now, or how he'd love to work alongside her. Just… *safety.* Benign concern for her well-being that he'd had throughout their whole friendship.

Are you thinking you'll *take it?* Just her. Alone. Again.

Anxiety rippled through her, followed by a wave of grief. It really was too much to hope that he'd want to settle down in the way she wanted to. His past all but guaranteed he couldn't love someone else fully, and she couldn't fault him for that.

Could she? Not entirely, but she *could* blame herself for letting her heart get so invested. He'd been honest from the start—this was temporary. But… but it didn't feel that way to her.

He made love to her more evenings than he didn't, and every night she fell asleep with his arms clasped tight around her bare waist.

He kissed her, his hands tangled in her hair.

He'd whispered that he loved her when he thought she was asleep.

Heat built behind her eyes. Had she made this whole thing up in her head?

No. She'd done everything right, from being vulnerable to doing good work.

Had he only been playing a part for the sake of the watchful eyes around the camp, the nights a way to scratch an itch and fill the time?

No… He'd never lead her on like that, would he?

Except she'd conveniently forgotten the second half of his admission of love from the night they'd first slept together—that it wasn't enough.

A commotion up ahead brought her back from her spiraling thoughts.

"Millie, have you seen Ben?" Ray asked, suddenly appearing beside her. His voice was a hushed whisper, but even if the crowd didn't know what was going on, they seemed to sense something was amiss. They were muttering to themselves and tension sat like a cloud above their heads.

"George's oldest? No, why?"

"He and his horse are missing."

Millie's veins turned to ice.

"I'm sure he's just wandered off to feed on the wild grass."

"Opie already checked. Can you run a perimeter check and see if he's gone back to the stables? Prince Philip would know to go back," Ray said, mentioning the horse they'd picked for the boy.

"Of course."

Millie used the reins to steer Tillamook toward the way they'd come when a shrill cry from behind her tore through her heart. *Ben*. Where was he? They'd been watching him, hadn't they?

Yes, until she'd been distracted by Dex's dismissal of her.

"Help!" Ben shouted. The plea had come from the cliffside that overlooked the ravine they'd just climbed out of.

Oh, no.

If Ben's horse got too close, they could both lose their footing on the scree field that lined the edge of the path.

Without giving it another thought, Millie kicked

her heels into Tilly's sides, whooping the horse to a gallop. Fear nipped at their heels as she raced toward the edge of the cliff, praying they weren't too late. Memories of the other patients she'd lost gnashed their teeth at her, urging her on. This life had to be different; otherwise what was the point of it all?

Dex's heart rate was damn near tachycardic. The pressure building on his chest prevented his lungs from drawing in a full breath, but he couldn't stop. Not when Millie was in danger.

Everything happened so fast, but at the same time like he'd been viewing the scene from afar in slow motion. First, he and Millie had agreed to tell Gale and Ray about their relationship. That was almost as good of news as the full-time contract. He hadn't wanted to dive into how he'd like nothing more than to take it and live with her for the rest of their lives, because he had the plan set up for after the ride; she'd see then just how he felt.

So he'd played it cool.

But then…

Gale had whispered something to Ray, who'd approached Millie at the back of the group of riders. He'd seen the worried twist of her mouth turn to an *O* of shock and fear he recognized. It was the same look she'd had on her face that night at Mac's bar.

Gale whispered what his concern was to Dex— the missing child and horse—just as Millie had turned back to the stables. Only a few feet into her turn, a distant cry came from the ravine they'd just meandered up. Millie broke her horse into a run, headed directly for the perilous edge of the cliff-side overlooking the ranch.

That's all it had taken for Dex to whip his horse, Ouray, into action. He had to catch Millie before it was too late.

"Please," he urged Ouray and whatever deities were listening in. "I need her to be safe." Fear trembled through him like an earthquake.

A few months ago, Dex would've worried about his own safety atop a horse, especially as he reined around the bushes and rocks blocking his direct path to Millie. But now he maneuvered like a professional rider—which he sort of was after all this time.

Not that he could enjoy the realization of how far he'd come. If he didn't get to Millie in time, he wouldn't be able to enjoy anything ever again.

Another cry tore through the erratic, quick beat of Dex's heart and the thump, thump of Ouray's hooves on the dry ground. As Dex rounded the corner, what he saw stopped his heart momentarily, but forced him to kick Ouray until the horse was racing at breakneck speed toward the rocky scree.

Millie was riding alongside Ben's horse, one arm linked around Ben's body as it dangled from the side of the saddle. Prince Philip wouldn't stop at the boy's urging, though he was going slow enough for Millie to unhook where the boy was tangled in the reins and move him over to her horse. She was still heading right for the loose rock that would send them all tumbling over the precipice until at the last minute, Ben safe in her arms, she veered into safety.

Dex caught them just as Millie slid to a stop on Tillamook and slipped off the saddle, Ben in her arms.

"He...he got spooked by somethin'," Ben sputtered through sobs. The boy protected his left arm against his chest as Dex breathed a sigh of relief. The boy and Millie were okay. His heart didn't get the message, though, rapidly slamming against his chest for several seconds until his breathing regulated. He kept the panic at bay, but barely.

He dismounted and fell to his knees next to Millie, who was inspecting Ben's arm and shoulder.

"It looks broken, and at the least, it's out of the socket."

Dex nodded.

"What's that mean?" Ben asked. "Will I need a cast?" Millie smiled softly as she felt around the boy's joint.

Dex resisted the primal urge to take her into his arms and never let her out of his sight again.

"Probably, but before that, I'm going to move your shoulder so it doesn't hurt anymore, okay? But it'll sting a little, Ben."

"That—that's okay. I'm brave and old enough to get a kitten. I can take it."

"I know you can." Millie counted to three and twisted Ben's arm into place. To his credit, the boy hissed in a sharp breath but didn't cry. "You did amazing, Ben. I need your flannel, Dex."

Dex handed it over, rubbing Millie's back in the

process, but she didn't seem to notice his presence. She fashioned a sling for Ben out of the shirt.

The rest of the group materialized over the hill and George ran to his son's side.

"Oh, God. He's okay?" he asked Millie. His jaw trembled but he was keeping his cool. Dex was proud of the man's progress. A month ago, this would have undone everything he'd worked for.

"He's going to be fine. He's actually one of the bravest patients I've ever had. Takes after his dad, I'm guessing."

Father and son beamed under Millie's praise and Gale helped them back onto George's horse for the ride back to the stables. George held tight to his son, but his muscles had otherwise relaxed.

"I'll follow in a sec to check in on them, but his arm needs to be x-rayed."

"You bet. I'll call ahead for an ambulance. I'm so sorry, George," Gale said, the set of his jaw more pronounced than ever. It wasn't his fault, though. Just a freak accident when Prince Philip spooked.

"Nah. Could've happened to anyone."

"Yeah! And it happened to *me*! I might get a cast for my friends to sign, Dad. Did you hear that?" Ben's glee made Gale chuckle as the pair moved away.

"That was pretty reckless, taking off like that," Dex said to Millie when the group, animated and tittering about the rogue horse and rescue, left the two of them behind to get Ben situated. Millie had promised to be right behind them but, of course, was trying to wrangle the horse that was now grazing at the edge of the grassy field as if nothing was amiss. "Are you okay?"

"I'm fine," she said, looking away from him. "And it wasn't reckless, it was my job. But you've never understood that, have you?"

"I'm sorry, but what's that supposed to mean?" He was the one who was supposed to be mad. She'd put herself in unnecessary danger. Again. She always would, wouldn't she?

His plan to tell her how he loved her, wanted to start a life with her, got fuzzy around the edges as the black tendrils of his anxiety snaked in.

Her gaze shot back to him. "It means you've never liked my choice in career, the places I choose to work, or hell, *me* for that matter."

Dex felt like the air had been stomped from his chest.

"Whoa, Millie. That's not true—"

"You're telling me you're fine with my time in the army, that DWB didn't scare the crap out of you?"

"It did, but only because of how much I care about you. And you're not doing DWB anyway, so what's this about?"

"It's about you refusing to acknowledge that my decisions aren't supposed to make *you* feel good. They're for *me*. *My* career, *my* life."

The finger she punched against her own chest might as well have been a fist thumped against his, the way her statement knocked the wind out of him. He loved this woman and she was blowing him off like the past three and a half months—hell, the past fifteen years—hadn't mattered at all.

"Doesn't it matter that I care that you have a life to come home to?"

And that I wish that home was with me, that I'd told you how I felt sooner?

"That doesn't give you the right to question my choices."

He sat back on his heels. "You're right."

Millie's face twisted into a scowl. She probably wasn't expecting him to agree, but there wasn't an ounce of her proclamation that didn't ring true. No matter how he felt about her, this was her life, not his.

"I've only ever cared about your well-being, but I can't control that any more than I can control the weather."

"No. You can't."

"So will you tell Ray you're taking the job?" It was an honest attempt at reconciling with her but she glared at him.

"Here we are again. What am *I* doing?" She spat the sentiment out like poison.

Wait…*what*?

"How did I screw this up? Please explain that, Millie."

Resignation seemed to sink her shoulders. "I…" She paused and looked back toward the camp. "I'm staying here, yes. The offer is amazing and I think I can do a lot of good. But I understand why it's too much for you."

"Too much *what*?" he asked. *Intimacy? Commit-*

ment? The damned thing of it was he wanted that with her. All of it, and to hell with what it meant.

"Dirt. Animals. Country living. You name it. We're not exactly swimming in metropolitan bliss here, Dex."

He smiled. He hadn't thought about all the trappings of the city in a while now. Not since waking up to Millie every morning became his new dream, the true thing that filled his heart. Fancy dining and shopping would never compare to the peace it brought him.

"Nah. But I can handle it." A gentle truce lifted the tension that had fallen since the accident and the ensuing argument between them.

Only when she wiped her hair from her forehead, did Dex see the smear of blood on her cheek and neck that had been hidden before. He traced it down and saw a deep gash on her shoulder, another along her arm.

What he could and couldn't handle blew away on the breeze that had picked up.

"You're bleeding," he whispered. A chill raced across his skin as she shrugged him off.

"I'm fine." The gentle armistice between them shattered and her wall shot back up, locking him out. Her gaze darted to the gnarled bushes she'd raced through without thinking, and his chest clenched again, reminding him that, with Millie in his life, a panic attack was never fully off the table. Traveling around the world or not, she would always court danger, wouldn't she?

And he'd always have to reckon with what that

meant for him. He knew what he wanted, but was he strong enough to keep it?

"Jesus, Mil. You could've been seriously hurt. Can you at least acknowledge that? For me?"

"For *you*?" she hissed. "I'm sorry, but I didn't think of *you* when Ben's horse took off. I thought of my job as a trauma physician and a patient in distress. And it's a good thing I did. That horse wasn't stopping and that cliffside wasn't getting any farther away."

Her breaths came in shallow gulps and her eyes watered. But that didn't stop her from shooting him a withering stare.

"Are you mad at me?" he asked. "Because I care?"

"It's not that you care, it's that you only seem concerned about whether or not my physical self is okay. Not if my heart hurts or what I'm think-ing about, or what my concerns for the future are."

"I listened while you told me what your plans are."

"Exactly. *My* plans. What *I'm* doing next. You didn't even say if it was something you'd consider, only that you can handle the dirt. But what about me, Dex? Can you handle *me*?"

That was the million-dollar question. His grand plan to share his feelings said yes, but that it was easy enough to put off when his anxiety flared up said maybe not.

God, did he want to, though.

"I'm here right now, aren't I?"

He cringed at his answer. *Way to be defensive, big guy.*

"Yep. Well said. You've always been a here-and-now guy."

"Oh, come on. I've been by your side for fifteen years, Millie. Doesn't that count for something?"

"It did until you told me I didn't matter to your future."

"When did I say that?" Dex stood up and paced before he was tempted to give in to the compulsion to clean and dress Millie's wounds. To wrap her up and care for her and about her until his last breath.

"When I told you about the contract with *both* our names on it and you asked what *my* plans were. There's never been a *we* or *us*, has there?"

Dex sighed, tossing his head back and swallowing a scream. He'd kept quiet on the ride to buy time till he could talk to her under the perfect conditions he'd drummed up with wine, an ocean view and his declaration speech carefully rehearsed.

But…maybe it was a good thing this was happening now, more organically. He'd always courted control, so maybe if he could let go a little…

"I'm trying, Millie. I've been talking to you, opening up to you in a way I never have with anyone else." He exhaled and let it all go. "I… I love you, Millie."

Her eyes grew wide, but she didn't relax her arms.

"Love means loving who I am, Dex. Not who you want me to be."

"I agree, and I do. I know I can't change you, and it might take a second to adjust how I think about our future, but the love I feel for you matters more than anything else."

Her face, her smile, her eyes lit up for the briefest of moments before they fell.

"It does, but as you so delicately pointed out before, it only matters if I choose jobs and situations you think are safe, that you agree with. Otherwise, you won't be okay, will you?"

"That's not fair, Millie. You know what I've been through in my life. You know what those kinds of risks—the kinds you take every day—do to trigger my past."

"I do. And I know you've been spouting that party line for a decade and a half without doing the work to get past your history. A couple months in a health spa won't fix you if you won't confront your fears. Look at those men and women down there. They've braved what I have and worse and they're ponying up and digging deep. You don't think they'd love to use their trauma as an excuse to never get close to anyone again?"

She finished her speech, breathless and heaving. Ten or more feet separated them now, but it might as well have been the breadth of the ravine below for as distant as he felt to Millie in that moment.

"You don't get it, Mil. What I've been through, who I've lost along the way—it's not fixed overnight. But I'm doing it, I'm making things better in the only way I can. Then you go and race toward a cliff and I—"

"You what? Because you aren't my therapist or

my father. You can't tell me not to take risks when it's for my *job*, Dex."

The thing about it was…she wasn't wrong. He'd been hiding behind his wounds for too long. Maybe it was time for him to pull out the ace he'd been holding up his sleeve—literally. His way to show he'd changed, that he'd thought of their future. No point in saving it for that afternoon…

It was now or never.

His heart pumped wildly as he slipped the bracelet he'd fashioned out of twine from one of the riding blankets off his wrist. He undid the knot, slipped off a ring and bent on one knee.

"Millie, will you marry me?"

"*Wha…? What*?"

"I do love you and I want to be better for you. Please accept this ring as proof I want the best for you."

His hopes were dashed completely when she shook her head, her eyes brimming with moisture. She hadn't even glanced at the one-and-a-half-carat diamond surrounded by a rose gold braid that reminded him of the braid she kept in Tilly's mane.

"Get up, Dex."

"Does that mean—?"

"Are you serious? It means no, Dex. I won't. And not because I don't love you. Because I do. More than almost anything. But I've been *not enough* or *too much* my whole life, and I can't go into the best thing that's ever happened to me worrying if being myself will trigger who *you* are. Because I love the person you are as well as who you're becoming, and

I wouldn't want you to be anyone different. Even for me. I'll take the job and you're free to go back to whatever safe career you want. We can tell Ray and Gale we've split up."

A figure rose up on the horizon behind Millie, who winced as she inspected the gashes on her shoulder and arm.

"Millie—" Dex tried.

"Stop. It doesn't matter, Dex." She shook her head and wouldn't meet his gaze as he tried to stop her from continuing. Ray was right behind her, but she hadn't noticed him. "Let's just get through this stint and then we can get back to where we were three months ago—"

"*Millie*—" he tried again, shaking his head more insistently, but she ignored him.

"Leave it alone. We can stop pretending to be anything more than just friends who needed a job. This relationship, though fun while it lasted, was fake from the start. It's time I realized that and let you go."

"Oh, Millie."

Ray gasped and Millie whipped around, scarlet covering her skin like a sheer red blanket.

"Ray," she whispered, and finally the tears that had been building along her bottom lid fell, staining her shirt. Their marriage might be fake, but all Dex wanted was to hold her. Even though it was too late. The damage was done in more than one way.

"Ray, that's not what I meant," she said, crying. Ray turned around and rode back to the stables and Millie broke down in sobs.

Dex inhaled, then sighed out a breath of instant shame and regret as he gazed up at Ray's back, praying that their friend—and boss—hadn't understood Millie's admission for what it was. But the set of his jaw, the steeliness of his gaze before he'd left said Ray had heard every single word.

And he wasn't happy about it.

CHAPTER THIRTEEN

MILLIE SWALLOWED THE regret as deep into her throat as she could shove it, but it didn't matter. It filled all the empty spaces in her and showed no signs of relenting. Nor should it. She'd messed up so badly and in so many ways.

On top of how horrible she felt? She'd made Ray feel that way, too. And that was worse. Way worse.

He'd actually gasped with surprise, but then a cold stare had captured his expression, holding it hostage until they all got down to the camp. Things had calmed down but all Millie wanted to do was drop Prince Philip off at the barn to be checked out, then peek in on Ben to see how the boy was faring.

What she had to do instead, as a result of blowing up her future with her callous carelessness, was pass Prince Philip off to Opie and follow Ray to where Gale was finishing up a report with the EMTs.

It felt like she was fourteen again and waiting for the principal to issue her sentencing for throwing food in the lunchroom.

While they waited for Gale to wrap up, Millie had plenty of time to consider her crummy life choices up to that point. The army had been a good job for a while, but she'd stuck with it until she came out the other side changed, unrecognizable and damaged all thanks to chasing a ghost of a family that would always disappear on her. Then there was the lie that she'd married her best friend, a poor decision that had too many ramifications, including the real relationship that had sprouted as a result of the fake one. Of course, it meant she'd had to maintain the lie to keep up appearances and in doing so, irrevocably hurt people she deeply cared about.

Yeah, she wasn't batting a thousand. Not even close.

Dex squirmed next to her.

"What?" she asked. "What is it now?"

"I do love who you are, Millie. It's just that if you get hurt again—"

"Dex, I could get hurt walking down the street in LA. It's a risk of being alive, that I could be injured, or worse. I can't hide from it."

"But you don't have to run toward it, either."

"No, I don't. That's my choice. But in making a different one, you run other risks, like not truly loving anyone." She closed her eyes against new tears that built, warm and hot behind her lids. "I don't think I can take this job anymore," she whispered. "If it's even still on the table. I'll give my notice now and beg DWB to take my late application."

"Why would you do that?"

"Because I can't keep living with you like this. It isn't real and it's only going to break my heart when we part ways at the end of this."

"Please just finish the six-month contract with me, Millie. What harm would it do?"

"You have the gall to ask me what *harm* it would

do? When you have absolutely no plans to stick it out with me aside from a proposal that seemed more like a desperate attempt to get me to stop chasing kids on horseback?"

"It wasn't desperate. I had a plan—"

"Of course you did. And plans change, Dex. That's part of life. Holding onto control never works."

"I know. And yet… I *want* to make plans with you."

"Well, I hate to be the one to point it out to you, Dex, but if we stick it out, I'm going to do everything in my power to help my patients, even if it makes you uncomfortable."

"I know that, believe me. And I'll be there for you if you'll let me. But you know how hard it is for me to accept change in my life. It was all I had when I was—"

"A kid. I do know that. But you're not a kid anymore, Dex. You're not risk-averse, you're stuck."

Dex's gaze dropped to his feet. "I didn't tell you about being homeless."

"Wait, what?"

"There was a year of my life I almost didn't survive. I was on the streets—twice, actually—because no one would take a teen boy with my foster-care track record into their home."

She gasped again, then shook her head.

"When?" she asked. She moved to hold his hand, but he kept it just out of reach.

"When I was a teen. I lived under a bridge for most of it, a park for the rest. The first winter I almost lost body parts to frostbite." Tears welled up in her eyes but he made no move to comfort her. "It's why I won't camp, why I like nice things— because I never had them before. But you—you make me want to forget my past entirely. I'm better with you."

"You never told me," she whispered.

"How could I? Even with your past, you had it all together."

"No, I didn't. But I didn't hide behind my past, either. You never trusted me enough to tell me the worst part of your life, even when you know what I've been through."

"I'm sorry, Millie. I just—"

"You just what?" Her gaze turned steely. "We only worked when you could control the variables. But that isn't love. You waited fifteen years to tell me something that would let me in. What else are you hiding from me, Dex?"

He snorted a laugh that surprised her. None of this was funny.

"Nothing."

"What?" she insisted. Her heart hurt, not just because this was ending, but because the man she loved had been through so much he'd kept to himself. No wonder he hadn't healed.

"Did you mean what you said back there?"

"Which part?" she asked. Millie's eyes were set on the cabin door in front of them, her heart somewhere near her stomach, in pieces.

"You know what part. You love me."

"I do. And?"

*Don't look at him. You can't if you want to make
it out of this with any shred of dignity.*

But Dex's finger hooked her chin and turned her
to face him.

"And I love you, too. Dammit, Millie, I have for
my whole adult life if I'm being honest with myself. We can make this work. If you can just be
patient—"

Heat built behind Millie's eyes but she'd cried all
the tears she had on the ride back to camp.

"I've *been* patient. And nothing's changed."

"How can you honestly say that? *Everything* has
changed."

And then she did it. She made the mistake of
raising her gaze to meet his. She was met with
searing liquid gray-blue pools that reflected the
depth of her feelings back to her. In the middle of
the pools was just what she'd feared—*love.*

It had been all she'd hoped for from Dex since
they'd met, but when he gave a voice to his own
trauma and how she reopened those wounds just by
being herself, well... How could she let him love
her when it would kill him with a thousand tiny
papercuts every time she did something risky or
dangerous in the scope of her work as a physician?

Wasn't that gross negligence in the extreme?

"Who you are, fundamentally at your core,
hasn't." She touched his chest as she said this, regretting it immediately. It'd been her pillow, her
rock and her passion for months now and touch-
ing it only reminded her of what she was walking
away from.

"Haven't I been growing from that person every day since we came here? I don't need the ritz or glam I've cultivated. Heck, I've even given up hair gel and shaving, for crying out loud." He smiled, but she wasn't in the mood. "Millie, I've been working on getting over my triggers every damn day."

"And I'm so happy you are, as a friend and a physician. But when I got hurt today, you reverted right back to a man who only seems to care about my physical well-being."

"Again, not true. I proposed to you, for eff's sake." The pain in his eyes shot through her armor to her heart.

Her chin fell, and she winced at the pain that shot from her shoulder down her arm.

"No, you tried to give me a ring, Dex. There's a difference."

He took her hand in his, and the heat that passed between their palms couldn't be ignored. "I want to let you in. I have, Millie, already. But I want to learn how to love you better, too. You mean so much to me."

And you mean everything to me.

Her heart screamed what her mouth couldn't say.

They loved each other fiercely, and that was the greatest tragedy of all. Because love wasn't enough this time. She couldn't love him into letting her be who she was and wanted to be. Her love couldn't teach him how to let go when he thought it meant he should cling tighter.

Just then, the door to the cabin opened and Ray

came out. His jaw had loosened, but his gaze was still as steely as his fiancé's.

"Millie, can we speak with you?" he asked.

"Not Dex?"

Ray shook his head. "We'd like to talk to him separately."

Millie gulped but nodded. "Okay." She shot Dex a longing glance filled with all the things she couldn't say.

That she loved him and always would.

That no other person would ever mean as much to her.

And a final pronouncement that succeeded in shattering her heart: that walking away from him was the biggest act of love she could give him—because it would save him, but ruin her.

Dex's foot tapped out a tattoo of regret that was only matched by his rapidly beating pulse. As a physician, he'd agree he was in distress. As a man in love, he knew it was more than that. He was heartbroken and filled with shame.

He'd let Millie go without telling her what his heart had been mumbling to him for months now.

I'm safe with you, *Millie.*

It wasn't that he couldn't love anyone without worrying he'd lose them, or didn't let them in because his dad died when he was a child. It's because no one in his life had ever allowed him to feel safe enough to open his heart fully. Until her. Until Millie.

But parsing through that realization—and that it

came too late—would have to wait until he'd finished talking to Ray and Gale. Millie had left half an hour prior, out the back door of the guys' cabin. She'd walked, head down, toward their bunkhouse without glancing back at him before shutting the door behind her.

No word about what was said behind the closed doors, no clue as to her emotional state. All he'd wanted to do was run to her—a pull as strong and natural as the coastal tides—but that wasn't in the cards. He needed to be where he was and make amends with his friends and bosses before he could make things right with Millie. At least he had a view of their bunkhouse from the window to his left.

He hadn't seen her leave, so that was something, an infinitesimal thread of hope that he still had time to fix this.

"Ben's okay, though?" he asked Gale.

"He is. Dr. Tyler-Sh—I mean, Dr. Tyler—is consulting with the pediatric doc at the local clinic and will keep us updated, but it looks like a bad sprain and not a break. We're really lucky."

"We are." Dex exhaled the half a breath he'd kept in since the boy had gone missing.

"Obviously, Ben's lucky, too, but I meant that Dr. Tyler was there when she was. If she hadn't gone after him…" Gale paused and looked to Ray, who gave his partner a look of pure love. Dex only recognized it because he'd been staring at Millie that way since he'd met the woman. "If she hadn't got-

ten there when she did, this would have been in-
finitely worse."

Dex nodded, then let his gaze fall to the floor.
"She's amazing."

Maybe if he hadn't been so obtuse, so wrapped
up in what he *thought* was the biggest problem—
her getting hurt—he'd have realized the truth. Her
risks helped people who couldn't help themselves.
Without her, so many people's lives would have
been worse, if not cut short. His included. And he'd
effed up the best thing that had happened to him
because it took him too damned long to realize that.

Well, that and because he still didn't know what
to do with that information.

"I'm glad you're finally figuring this out," Ray
said.

Dex lifted his head, surprised by the comment.
What shocked him more was the hesitant smile
on Ray's face. Dex looked at Gale, who was smiling, too.

"Wait, *what*?" was all Dex could get out.

"I mean, we hoped when you two finally started
hooking up that it wouldn't take you long to realize you really were meant for each other, but what
could we do except stand by and hope you didn't
bungle things," Gale said.

"Which you did," Ray chimed in, complete with
an eye roll that would make Millie proud.

"You—you *knew*?"

"Oh, Doc. We may be simple cowboys, but we're
not stupid."

"But—but *how*?"

"First of all, there wasn't any record of a Dr. Tyler-Shaw. If you look at our contracts, they're written out to your actual names. Then there's the way you looked at each other."

"How was that?" Dex couldn't recall a time he hadn't looked at Millie like he did when they spooned, locked in an embrace after making love.

"Like you wanted to bone but couldn't."

Dex laughed then, deep and long.

"Damn. Who knew we were that transparent?"

"You have no idea," Ray said.

Dex ran a hand through his hair. "Does she know you were aware this whole time?"

"She does."

Gale narrowed his gaze at his fiancé, then shook his head. What weren't they saying?

"Then why'd you let us take the gig?"

Gale shrugged. "If you wanted to saddle yourselves to a small bunk in the middle of nowhere together, that was your business. When you got here, we actually bet you wouldn't last a week," he said. "We had another couple on standby."

"Yeah, we almost didn't," Dex admitted, recalling their fight about the horse-riding part of the job. Now he couldn't imagine life without the gentle beasts. Or Millie. Or Ray and Gale, for that matter.

"I meant *you*."

Dex chuckled. "That was probably a safe bet."

"But when we saw you two together, we realized that no piece of paper could define what you two had. You're best friends," Gale said. Dex just nodded.

"Soulmates," Ray challenged.

"Not anymore. I seriously effed things up and she said she was giving her notice."

Ray and Gale shared a look that said Dex was missing something.

"Well, we may have convinced her to stick around a little while so you have time to fix whatever mess you made. But she does need some time alone, without you around, to process things, so I—"

"We," Ray interjected.

"*We* think you should use that time wisely. Get help—real help—healing from your past and being a hundred percent ready if you want to win her back. We'll help with the former, but you have to put in the work."

The surprise that flashed hot on Dex's skin felt a lot like embarrassment. It came after the sting of hearing she needed time away from him, but he didn't blame her a bit for that.

"Of course. But…why would you help me when we lied to you?"

"Well, we were more concerned that you were lying to yourselves than to us. We got two expert physicians and good friends whose troubled love story helped us see the happy-ever-after of our own."

Hmm. Dex gave that some thought. If he was that transparent from the beginning—enough that his bosses were less pissed about the lie than they were about him screwing this all up—maybe there was more hope than he thought. For more than just him and Millie, but their professional futures as well.

"Where do I start?"

"We'd love it if you agreed to keep working with us for starters," Gale said.

Millie had shared the details of the contract—it was as sweet a deal as he could ask for. "Of course. I'm just glad that offer's still on the table."

"Then, you start Operation: Get Her Back," Ray quipped. "With our help, of course. Because we saw how you flubbed it up when left to your own devices."

"*Only*," Gale said, "after we know you're serious about her. About why you want to pursue this. And that you're ready for what loving her would mean. And after you meet us each night to dive into how to keep that work up."

Dex just smiled, locks clicking into place in his head and heart, syncing them for the first time in, well, forever.

Working on himself was the most radical act of love he could give to Millie. And she was worth coming out of the shadows for.

"Okay. I'm in. I love this woman something fierce and she's worth the work."

"Good. But if you screw this up and we lose two friends *and* colleagues, I'll put a hex on you for the rest of your life."

Dex laughed as he got up and strode toward the door. He had work to do and not a lot of time to pull it together. The plans had been starting to come together in his head for two months, since he and Millie had first woken up together and he'd—slowly—come to the realization he wanted to be able to do that every morning for the rest of his life. He'd just needed time to get out of his own way and recognize the reason behind his need for control. It wasn't the lack of love from his childhood or even needing to control Millie's safety.

It was finding a place *he* felt safe.

And wouldn't you know it, the "place" wasn't a place at all—it was a person. A tall, curvy, brilliant, quick-witted woman with long curly auburn hair. It wasn't that she made him a better person—that would be too selfish a reason to love and pursue her. It was that he became the person he was capable of being when they worked together. When he made her laugh. When he listened to her dreams and they fueled his own. When he explored her body and gave his up to her in return.

Now that he knew all that—and Ray and Gale were going to help him learn how to keep his fears at bay—he could be the man Millie needed.

"Ray, if I don't get this right and I lose Millie, there's no spell on earth that'll be as devastating as how I'll make myself feel. But once we're at a place you're comfortable with me pursuing her again, I could actually use your help with one phase of my plan."

Ray clapped and bounced on the balls of his feet.

"I'd better be invited to the actual wedding," he cooed.

"Hell. You'll be my best man if you'll take the gig."

"Excuse me," Gale said, shooting Dex a withering stare from under his bushy cowboy brows.

"Gale, I know I speak for Millie, but if she accepts my proposal, we'd actually love for you to officiate."

Gale, the perpetually unemotional one of the group, wiped at his eyes and sniffed.

"Um, I could do that. Sure." He wrapped Dex in a bear hug and squeezed. Ray joined in and a calming warmth washed away most of the guilt sitting at the base of Dex's throat.

Dex pulled away; his smile evaporated like the morning fog off the Cambria coast.

"But seriously, guys. I'm deeply sorry for lying to you both. It isn't excusable no matter what you were aware of or not. Friends don't lie, and I can promise that won't happen again."

"We know why you did it. I'm just glad it brought you to us. Hearts and Horses is better for having you both. Now, let's get our girl back."

That was all Dex needed to hear to put the final touches on a lifelong plan to show Millie not only how much she meant to him, but how he'd be able to care for her heart, if she'd only give him another chance. It might take some time to pull off, but when forever was stretched out in front of him, what did a few days matter?

CHAPTER FOURTEEN

DEX STRUMMED THE GUITAR, glancing over at Millie through the dancing fire. Each time a spark floated up with the breeze, she'd track it, the ember reflecting off her emerald irises. Occasionally, she'd meet his gaze and heat not from the bonfire would glow on her cheeks.

He longed to brush the space where the red bloomed on her skin, feeling the warmth for himself. But it wasn't time for that yet. His fingers itched, but he steadied them with even breaths, born of patience.

There was only one more chance to get this right.

They'd come to a gentle impasse the past few weeks, one that required very little of either of them. Neither one had said anything, since words were what got them in trouble in the first place. But work and their friends and patients had consumed them, easing the hurt. If he was watching from the outside and had to put a label on it, he'd say they were tentative friends, with an echo of love pulsing between them. Probably much the way they'd looked when Gale and Ray had sussed them out all those months ago.

She'd moved into the spare room at Gale and Ray's and their therapy sessions had been split so he rarely saw her anymore. Of course, she stopped wearing the gold band he'd given her all those months ago and he couldn't say he liked that development, either, not when he'd gotten so used to seeing it as their tether to one another.

But he wouldn't be giving it back anytime soon, either—he'd save his grandmother's band for the actual wedding. The one burning a hole in his jeans—the Tilly braid, he called it—would make a damn fine replacement until then.

All he wanted was to see his commitment to her worn out loud for all to see.

Which was why it had been damn near impossible for Dex to keep his true feelings to himself as they wrapped up Family Weekend and got into their new routines, including his agreed upon nights of therapy with Gale and Ray.

They'd done wonders to give him techniques he'd never considered to work through his anxiety, but more importantly, because he trusted them, he was able to dig below the wounds of his youth and excavate them once and for all. Including his time without a home when he'd lived on the streets.

To be honest, he'd be keeping those sessions up regardless of how things went tonight.

"You doing okay?" Gale asked, scooting closer to Ray on their log bench.

Dex nodded. He was better than okay.

"He's nervous," Ray whispered.

That was only partly true.

In all honesty, his heart was simply impatient to start the rest of his life with a woman he loved as completely as he loved medicine, as he loved his job, as he loved his own growth. She was a part of him.

"Okay, guys. We ready?"

Ray's smile and vivacious nod spoke for his answer.

"Hell yes," Gale added.

With that, Dex got up and the crowd of first responders quieted. He strummed a chord on his guitar and they began a gentle humming that matched pitch. They harmonized beautifully, the gentle lap of the water on the sand as background vocals.

He'd been taking secret guitar lessons since Millie—only half joking—mentioned wanting a long-haired man who'd play her songs on his guitar. He'd give that woman anything she wanted, even if it meant learning their unofficial proposal song from their fake relationship over the past month.

From the corner of his eyes, he saw the shock on Gale and Ray's face. They didn't know this was part of the plan—him singing, yes, but the patients who'd been a part of his and Millie's journeys? He'd kept that quiet. In the beginning, he hadn't been sure what sharing the truth about him and Millie would do to the trust he'd built with them, but he'd underestimated his patients for what would be the last time. They were forgiving and supportive—more than he had a right to expect. Involving them in the proposal had been Reese's idea, one he'd agreed to right away.

Even though it made him happy to see the love and joy on his friends' faces, it only half registered with him. His gaze and hopes for the future were pinned to the soft glow on Millie's face, to the curious expression drawn on her lips as she tried to figure out what was happening.

Her eyes darted from Dex to the others, then back again, but when Dex broke out in the lyrics to "Unchained Melody," a smile erupted, scrunching her cheeks and eyes in the way he found wholly adorable and altogether sexy.

He and the crowd circled Millie, then walked out of the fire circle. He kept her in his periphery, watching to see what she'd do, and thankfully, she got up with Ray and Gale and followed them. Dex led the group around the rocky outcrop blocking a hidden bay Ray had shown him a couple weeks prior on the moonlit ride on this same beach.

Dex handed off his guitar to Gale, who kept the melody playing as Dex turned to face the entrance to the bay. When Millie came around the corner, he walked over to her, delighting in the look in her eyes.

The dozens of solar-powered candles he'd set up with the help of Gale and some of the other staff sparkled and shimmered off the water and her deep green eyes. Her hair was wild and free and the gentle breeze moved her curls in a sway that hypnotized him. But the most arresting part of her features was the way she'd drawn her bottom lip between her teeth—her I'm-deliriously-happy look.

Seeing that settled the frenetic beat of his heart against his chest. His one goal was to make her nibble on that bottom lip every day of the rest of her life, and he was already batting a thousand.

"Hey there, pretty lady," he said, and she laughed, her head thrown back in joy. Hopped up on pain-killers, he'd said the same thing to her when she'd checked in on him in the ICU all those years ago, just hours after his accident.

"Hey there, killer," she replied, harkening back to her own reply fifteen years ago.

"Can I talk to you a moment?" he asked. She nodded, and he continued, "You're right, Millie. Your life is too dangerous, too outside my comfort zone."

"What—" she started, but he shook his head.

"But the thing is, *love* means being constantly outside one's comfort zone, no matter what else is safe. And make no mistake, Millicent Rebekah Tyler. I love the hell out of you."

She smiled, but it didn't reach her eyes. She was still concerned, and had a good right to be.

"Loving you is my heart walking around outside this body and to be honest, I don't mind you holding onto it for the rest of your life. You'll protect it. I know that much now, thanks to Gale and Ray." He smiled back at them and Ray sighed like he did whenever anything romantic happened.

"I gave my heart to you a long time ago and even knowing it's a sunk cost if you turn me down isn't enough to make me want it back. I only want *you*. And not just because you make me better—which you do. But because you make everyone around you better, because you're the light in so many dark places. I love your energy and want to orbit around you for a while just so I can watch you glow. But you need to know one thing before any of that can happen."

"What's that?" she asked. The edges of her eyes were etched with laugh lines. All he wanted was to deepen them.

"I've done the work. And I'll keep on doing it so you never have to worry about being your beautiful, amazing, brave self ever again."

"Okay," she whispered.

"Millie, will you trust me with your heart and know I'll only ever help it chase down its deepest desires? Will you let me chase you around while you save and change lives?"

"What about all the risks loving me poses?"

"They aren't risks, Millie. They're bonds and connections I'd never trade for all the safety without them. As long as you want me to be, I'll be there beside you, even if it's hard at times."

"But I don't want you changing for me, either."

"Too late. I've been changing cell by cell since you pulled me out of the car and kept saving my life every day since. And that's not a bad thing. Nor should it be any kind of pressure on you," he added when her smile fell just enough for him to notice. "It'd happen with or without you in my life simply because you being you inspires me to reach for all my potential."

"Me, too," chimed Ray.

"Same here," Gale added.

The whole chorus of veterans and first responders all added similar sentiments, making Millie laugh.

"See? That's the effect you have on others, Mil. And I want to give that back to you every amazing day of our lives if you'll have me."

"If I'll have you?"

He knelt in the sand.

"At the risk of being rejected again, I want to know if you'll marry me and let me make you bite your lip like that every day for the rest of our lives."

He gestured behind him and the crowd of their friends and patients parted, showing off a towering sandcastle that was crafted to resemble their bunkhouse on the ranch set on a hill of sand and shells, two sand characters depicted in the window, holding hands.

Along the base of the cabin castle, he had written *Marry me, Millie Tyler* in shells and seaweed. Her eyes twinkled and gleamed in a way that had nothing to do with the candles outlining the sculpture.

"You used both my names," she said. He nodded. "It's just like the story we told a few months ago." Her voice was distant, like she was a thousand miles away. "It's perfect."

"It's what you deserve."

She walked through the shell-and sand-sculptures, then reached down and touched the top of the castle, a soft smile playing on her lips while the patients hummed the song and Gale strummed the chords along with them. Peace settled on her features and when she turned to face him, he was knocked across the chest with emotion.

Good grief, she was beautiful, wasn't she? His opposite, yet equal partner.

"So, what do you say, Millie? Will you do me the honor of becoming the second Dr. Shaw?"

She shook her head.

"I don't think so," she said. Dex's smile fell along with his heart.

Well, damn. He honestly hadn't expected that. Not a second time in a row.

"Oh, okay." He started to get up, but she joined him kneeling in the cool, damp sand.

"I'd rather be the first Dr. Tyler-Shaw."

He looked up and met her gaze. It took a second for his brain to catch up to his heart and process the warmth spreading from his chest outward.

"So, you'll marry me, Tyler?"

"I will, Shaw, if you're sure."

"Sure? Hell, I should have married you fifteen years ago when you pulled me out of that vehicle. Well," he said, grinning at the look of shock on her face, "after you cleaned and dressed my injuries, of course."

"Oh, Dex. We might not have been ready then, but I'm more than ready now."

"As am I. I can't wait to make all your dreams come true."

"Don't you know?" Millie asked, her eyebrows frowning even though her smile stayed glued in place. "You already have."

He dove into her, all but knocking her on her backside, and wrapped her as tightly as he could in his arms. Gale, Ray and the others whooped and hollered, but he was only vaguely aware of them leaving the beach to give them the privacy they needed to celebrate this momentous occasion.

"I love you, Millie Tyler, and I'm going to make you the happiest woman on the planet."

"I love you, Dexter Shaw, and I think I just might let you."

When he kissed her this time, it was with a promise fifteen years in the making. And it was a promise he couldn't wait to keep every day of the rest of his life.

EPILOGUE

A year later

MILLIE GAZED OUT the window, over the ranch that had become home to her and Dex over the past year and a half. Two days a week, they commuted into Mercy to use their services in a new partnership with their trauma and psych wings, but the rest of the time they lived and worked and played in South Central California. Hearts and Horses took them on full-time and with the influx of physicians and new programs, they'd more than doubled their outreach. Owen Rhys, the plastic surgeon from Mercy, even did consults for the injured first responders out at the ranch.

It was a beautiful time, but not near as beautiful as what lay in front of Millie, actually and metaphorically. The gazebo, flower-lined aisle and horses with flowers in their manes were physical manifestations of her excitement over her future, as were the tulle dresses hanging in her old bunkhouse suite.

Since they were staying on and partnering with Gale and Ray now that the couple were back from their honeymoon in Turks and Caicos, she and Dex had had a small cabin built on the back of the property. So, for now, the bunkhouse was an elaborate bridal suite in which she, Ray and Reese used to prep for the big day.

She'd wanted a few minutes alone in the bunk-house, a reminder of where she and Dex had first fallen in love, first decided to test the stability of their friendship. Could it hold a big love?

Oh, how it could. And when things had grown heavy—like when her stepmother had died suddenly of a heart attack—their love had just expanded to carry them.

They really had grown so much over the course of the past year. Dex had learned that he was worthy of love and that control and safety weren't to be found in places, but in himself and those he cared for.

And Millie? Well, she'd learned how much adventure could be found in the love of another, in the exploration of the ordinary, in the depth of a heart. She didn't need to travel to get it. Not all the time, anyway. She *was* rather looking forward to her and Dex's honeymoon, though.

A month driving up the Pacific Coast Highway, through Canada, and into Alaska, where they'd spend the remaining time in a small cabin on a remote island off the coast of Kenai? Yeah, that would be nice.

Someone knocked and she smiled. "Come on in," she said, expecting Ray and Reese, her two best friends and both of whom were standing up for her in the small intimate wedding in less than an hour. She'd finagled Ray over to her side by promising he could wear a kilt and Dex had agreed that was far more appropriate than the stiff outfits on the groom's side of the aisle. For all Dex had changed, she kind of liked that he'd kept his penchant for the finer things, especially since he dragged her along for shopping trips and lavish weekend trips around the southwest that filled her heart with joy.

She turned around, putting a final layer of gloss on her lips.

"Oh, my goodness, Dex. You shouldn't be here," she said, though her heart argued otherwise. She'd been counting down the seconds until she got to marry her best friend.

His eyes were on the ground, intentionally not looking at her in her off-the-shoulder white lace dress. Even with his chin tipped, though, she caught the smile that damn near arrested her heart every time he flashed it on her.

"I can go…" he said, his voice laced with mischief.

She laughed. "No. I want you here."

"Can I look at you, or is that bad luck?"

Millie made her way over to him and tilted his chin so he could meet her gaze. He smiled, his eyes watering as he took her in, from peep-toe heel to the long waves she'd somehow miraculously tamed with a half updo.

"You're stunning," he whispered. "Tell me I'm really lucky enough to be marrying my best friend who's also sexy as hell."

"I'll just say that if you meet me by the altar in an hour, you might just *get* lucky. Every night until you tell me otherwise." She winked, her bottom lip drawn between her teeth, and he laughed.

"I'll *never* tell you otherwise." Dex's face grew serious. She noticed the telltale way he nibbled on the inside of his cheek, something he did when he was thinking about something. "Millie, I don't know if I ever thanked you properly."

"For what?"

"Saving my life."

"You did. Hundreds of times, love."

He pulled her into a deep kiss, his palms cupping her cheeks.

"Not on the day of the accident, though I'll never stop being grateful for that, either."

"What do you mean, then?"

He brushed his lips lightly over hers and tingles spread like fire through her veins. God, she hoped he would always have that effect on her.

"The day you agreed to try this," he said, gesturing to the infinitesimal space between their bodies. This time she reached up and pulled him down into her, their lips meeting in the space their hearts already shared. "The day you helped me realize what I needed to do to keep saving myself so I could be there for you."

"Then, in that case, thank *you*."

His brows quirked with curiosity.

"For saving my life, too. I never thought I'd know happiness like this, Dex. Not after all I've been through. I'll never stop being grateful for the life of love and family you've given me."

"And I'll never stop trying to make you happier than you are today."

The door slammed open and Ray burst inside.

"Excuse me!" he shouted, though his mustache couldn't hide the smile he wore. "You all might not stand on decorum, but I most certainly do."

"I'm just kissing my bride," Dex said, his eyes gleaming with joy and something saucier.

"Well, do it in front of God and everyone who showed up to see you two get hitched. Not before the wedding, for crying out loud. Now, shoo." He all but shoved Dex toward the door.

When he got to the doorframe, Millie called out to him, laughing, "I love you, Shaw. I'll see you at the altar."

"I'll be the one in the tux, Tyler. Time to put those long runs to use and hurry down the aisle to me. I can't wait to make you mine."

"Me, neither." She smiled as Ray shut Dex out of the suite. It was the last time in her life a door would be closed for her and the love of her life, her best friend.

She stood up an hour later, Ray and Reese on either side of her.

"Okay, you two, take me to get married. I have a groom waiting on me."

With that, she opened the door to her future, and it was as bright as anything she could have hoped for.

* * * * *

If you enjoyed this story, check out these other great reads from Kristine Lynn

Accidentally Dating His Boss
Brought Together by His Baby

All available now!